PRAISE FOR JESSICA DAY GEORGE'S

Tuesdays at the Castle series

"These kids are clever, as is George's lively adventure. May pique castle envy." —*Kirkus Reviews* on *Tuesdays at the Castle*

"This story puts an unexpected spin on the typical princess tale. Readers will root equally for crafty Celie and for her castle." —*Library Media Connection* on *Tuesdays at the Castle*

"There is a warmth here that is utterly irresistible."
—*BCCB* on *Tuesdays at the Castle*

"A charming, adventurous story with a spirit that will appeal to fans of Kate DiCamillo's *The Tale of Despereaux*. . . . *Tuesdays at the Castle* is all the more enjoyable for the intelligent, strong characters who dwell within its pages and castle walls." —Shelf Awareness on *Tuesdays at the Castle*

"There is plenty to charm readers in this second book in the series. . . . The Castle is a character in its own right, and readers will be fascinated to learn more about its history."
—*School Library Journal* on *New York Times* bestselling *Wednesdays in the Tower*

"A sweet, funny, sincere story in which siblings work together." —*Kirkus Reviews* on *New York Times* bestselling *Wednesdays in the Tower*

"Full of excitement, adventure, humor, and mystery." —*Random Musings of a Bibliophile* on *New York Times* bestselling *Wednesdays in the Tower*

"Lovely and engaging, this fantasy series continues to have wide appeal." —*Booklist* on *Thursdays with the Crown*

"Fans of the series will eagerly devour this latest installment." —*School Library Journal* on *Thursdays with the Crown*

WEDNESDAYS
in the Tower

Books by Jessica Day George

Dragon Slippers
Dragon Flight
Dragon Spear

Tuesdays at the Castle
Wednesdays in the Tower
Thursdays with the Crown
Fridays with the Wizards
Saturdays at Sea

Sun and Moon, Ice and Snow

Princess of the Midnight Ball
Princess of Glass
Princess of the Silver Woods

Silver in the Blood

JESSICA DAY GEORGE

BLOOMSBURY
NEW YORK LONDON OXFORD NEW DELHI SYDNEY

First published in the United States of America in May 2013
by Bloomsbury Children's Books
Original paperback edition published in May 2014
New paperback edition published in February 2017
www.bloomsbury.com

For information about permission to reproduce selections from this book, write to Permissions, Bloomsbury Children's Books, 1385 Broadway, New York, New York 10018
Bloomsbury books may be purchased for business or promotional use. For information on bulk purchases please contact Macmillan Corporate and Premium Sales Department at specialmarkets@macmillan.com

The Library of Congress has cataloged the hardcover edition as follows:
George, Jessica Day.
Wednesdays in the tower / by Jessica Day George.—First U.S. edition.
pages cm.
Sequel to: Tuesdays at the Castle.
Summary: After discovering a giant egg hidden in a newly created room of Castle Glower, Princess Celie agrees to care for the egg and the creature it hatches.
ISBN 978-1-59990-645-4 (hardcover) • ISBN 978-1-61963-051-2 (e-book)
[1. Fairy tales. 2. Castles—Fiction. 3. Princesses—Fiction.
4. Kings, queens, rulers, etc.—Fiction. 5. Griffins—Fiction.] I. Title.
PZ8.G3295We 2013 [Fic]—dc23 2013000262

ISBN 978-1-68119-219-2 (new paperback)

Book design by Donna Mark
Typeset by Westchester Book Composition
Printed and bound in the U.S.A. by Berryville Graphics Inc., Berryville, Virginia
2 4 6 8 10 9 7 5 3 1

For Baby Roo,
who has been my companion during
every moment of writing this book

Chapter 1

There are a lot of things that can hatch out of an egg. A chicken, for example. Or a dragon. And when the egg in question is the size of a pumpkin, and almost as orange, not to mention burning hot, you know that you're far more likely to get a dragon than a chicken. So when Celie found the egg—large, orange, and too hot to touch—lying in a nest of oddly vine-like moss in the new tower, she was convinced that it held a baby dragon. Where it had come from and what would happen when it hatched were two questions that she wasn't sure she wanted answered.

It was a Wednesday, so Celie didn't expect to find any new rooms in Castle Glower. The youngest of the Glower children, Princess Cecelia—Celie, to nearly everyone—knew the Castle better than any person living there, and thought she knew what to expect from it. The day before had been exciting enough, with the room with the bouncy floor being moved to the opposite end of the Castle, and a long room filled with exotic armor appearing just off the portrait gallery. One no longer had to climb through a fireplace to get to the bouncy room, though the door was inconveniently located in her father, King Glower's, study. And the Armor Gallery, as it had already been dubbed, was in the perfect place for such a thing, though the maids were nearly in revolt at the idea of having to clean and polish so many strangely shaped items.

As she left breakfast and went up the spiraling stairs to the schoolroom for her lessons, Celie wasn't thinking of finding anything more interesting that day. She was mostly hoping that she would be able to get a look at some of the new armor after her lessons. Her eldest brother, Bran, newly home from the College of Wizardry and now instated as the Royal Wizard, had assured the maids that they would not have to clean the Armor Gallery, because he didn't want anyone to touch the contents. At least some of the weapons had proved to have magic powers, and he wanted to figure out what everything did and how dangerous it was first. But Celie was sure he'd at least let her look at some of it, if she could get out of her lessons before dinner.

The schoolroom wasn't at the top of the spiral staircase.

Celie looked around. She was in a long corridor that she had never seen before.

She flipped open the leather satchel slung over her shoulder and pulled out her atlas, a detailed set of maps that she had been working on for years. At last she was nearly done with it, and had already talked to some of the Castle scribes about making copies for her family, but she wanted to get the latest changes in first. It helped that the Castle had not taken away any rooms in at least a month, though it had added a few rather interesting ones (including a second, smaller kitchen and the Armor Gallery), and moved several others. Celie's room seemed to be permanently fixed on the eastern side of the main hall, but Bran's room was now right next to it, and Lilah's was just beyond that, which made Lilah pout: she had previously been on an upper level with fantastic views from both windows.

Celie flipped through her collection of maps, but couldn't find anything that resembled this corridor. There were no doors along it, and the schoolroom was just *gone*, as was the old nursery. No one had used the nursery in years, of course, but they had stored their old toys and outgrown clothes in it. Celie found that map and crossed out the nursery, then put a question mark beside the schoolroom before hurrying along the corridor. She needed to find the schoolroom, both to correct her maps and to get to her lessons before Master Humphries had a fit.

At the end of the corridor was a wide flight of shallow steps. Celie could feel chill air moving down the stairs, as if a window at the top had been left open. Like many of the stairs in the Castle, these were oddly proportioned. Celie almost needed to take two steps on each riser, but they were only a few inches high, and it was awkward.

Fortunately there were only eight of them, and then she was stepping through a stone arch into a circular room with no roof.

The pale late-winter sun was shining down into the open room, and Celie stumbled as she walked forward, staring up at the thin wisps of clouds. The floor of the room sloped toward the middle like a bowl. In the middle of the bowl was a nest of moss and twigs, and in the middle of the nest was a gleaming orange egg. It was the same orange as a ripe pumpkin, and just as big as one. Celie gaped at it.

"Is that really an egg?"

Icy wind whipped through the uncovered windows and carried her words away. She took some careful steps forward and leaned over. She reached out a hand, wanting to knock on the shell. She imagined it would be cold and very hard, petrified from years of sitting in an open room.

But it wasn't cold. It was hot, almost too hot to touch comfortably.

Celie snatched her hand back and ran for the door. She hurried out the archway and down the shallow steps. In the corridor leading to the staircase there were several enormous tapestries, but she didn't stop to look at the details. She went back down the spiral steps and lurched to a confused halt on the next landing down.

Directly across from her was the schoolroom, just as it

always was. But for as long as she could remember, the schoolroom had been at the top of the spiral stairs, not halfway down. Hadn't it?

"Princess Cecelia!" Master Humphries came to the door of the schoolroom, looking impatient. "Where have you been? You are a quarter of an hour late!"

"I went up the stairs, but there's a new corridor there," Celie said. She pointed upward.

"I don't know what you're talking about," Master Humphries said, frowning. "Please come in, Your Highness. It is better that we begin late than not at all."

"But I think I should tell my brother," Celie said. "There's an egg—"

"An egg?" Master Humphries raised his eyebrows. "I am sure that Prince Bran can find eggs in the kitchen, if he is so inclined, for breakfast," her tutor said curtly.

"No, up there," Celie said, pointing again.

"There is nothing up there, Your Highness," Master Humphries said. He sighed. "Please do not use the Castle as an excuse. You of all people should be able to find your way around the Castle's vagaries in a timely fashion."

"But look!" Celie pointed more emphatically, looking up herself.

There was nothing above her but a smooth, gray stone ceiling. She felt a moment of dizziness as she discovered that she was now standing on the top step of the spiral staircase. The rest of the steps she had just come down, and the corridor above where she had found the tower and the egg, were gone.

"There was a new corridor," Celie said faintly. "And a tower with no ceiling. A nest. And an egg."

"But, Your Highness," Master Humphries said, taking her by the arm to lead her into the schoolroom, "it's Wednesday."

Chapter 2

A week later, and still Bran wouldn't let anyone touch the armor or weapons in the new gallery. One of the footmen had tried to help Bran move a suit of armor to a table for easier study, and the breastplate had sent a jolt of lightning through his hands that made them numb for hours afterward. That was when Bran had declared that until he was done inspecting everything, no one was allowed in the gallery unsupervised.

"Which breastplate was it?" Rolf said with great interest.

The younger of the Glower princes, he was the heir to the throne, as the Castle had decided on his tenth birthday. Despite his growing responsibilities, he was always up for some fun, and Celie was hoping he would find a secret way into the Armor Gallery and let her come as well.

"Never you mind," Bran said.

"What does that lance do?" Celie said.

She had her hands behind her back, and was leaning as close to a long golden lance as she dared.

"It shocks little girls who breathe on it," Bran said crossly.

Celie leaped back, but then she made a face at Bran. "Mean!"

"I'm here because Father sent me to ask you if you need anything," Rolf said importantly. "And also because I'm really hoping you'll give me first crack at any magical swords or helmets of invisibility." He rubbed his hands together eagerly.

"Yes, I need something, and no, you cannot have a magical sword," Bran said, making some notes in his notebook.

"What do you need?" Celie asked as she wandered over to look at a rack that held armor made of tiny overlapping wooden scales.

"I need Pogue Parry from the village, and to not be worrying that you'll touch something," Bran said. He sighed. "I'm not trying to be a bear, Cel," he said kindly. "But some of these things could probably kill you with a single touch."

Rolf whistled and put his hands behind his back.

"I just have one question," Celie said. "Well, two now: What do you need Pogue for, and are dragons real?"

Pogue had been invaluable when their parents and Bran had gone missing the summer before, but he was also an incorrigible flirt. When he wasn't being saucy with the village girls or fighting duels with their jilted suitors, he was often hanging around the castle, teasing Lilah.

"Pogue's a journeyman blacksmith," Bran reminded her. "I thought he could help me figure out if some of these things were forged by hand or made by magical means. And no, dragons aren't real."

"They've never been real? In the past, perhaps, and then they died off?"

"No," Bran said absently, squinting at some strange marks etched on the breastplate he was studying. "They're only legends. Always have been."

"So what kind of animal would lay an egg the size of a pumpkin?" Celie asked.

"That's three questions," Rolf pointed out.

"Is that a riddle?" Bran asked at the same time. "Nothing lays an egg that large. Not even the rocs in Grath."

"Rocks?" Rolf looked faintly alarmed. "The *rocks* lay eggs in Grath?"

"*Rocs*. No *k*," Bran clarified. "They're enormous, predatory birds. Ask Lulath about them; just make sure you send for Pogue first!"

Bran turned his back on Celie and Rolf, making it clear that he was going to ignore them while he continued his wizardly business. Rolf took Celie's elbow and they edged out of the gallery, being careful not to touch anything. Out in the corridor, Rolf breathed a sigh of relief.

"That's so odd," he said. "That whole gallery, just full of foreign weapons and armor . . ." He shook his head. "It looked like fun at first, but now I don't know what to think about it. Have you added it to your maps yet?"

"No," Celie said. "There's just so much lately . . ."

She didn't want to tell him that after her lessons, when she'd planned to sketch the Armor Gallery, she'd been trying to find a new corridor instead. One that could only be reached by a spiral staircase, and ended in a tower that contained a single giant egg. She had failed to find the corridor, and it had happened so fast, and had disappeared so swiftly, that she was half-convinced that it had all been in her imagination.

"Father was telling some of the councilors about your atlas," Rolf said. "I know he'd love to have a copy made, to show off. It could really come in useful for people who are visiting the Castle."

Celie felt herself blushing. "It's not done yet," she protested. She'd wanted to make a gift of it to the family, but she wasn't sure how she felt about councilors and strangers looking at her sketches and notes.

"Well, I don't know if it will ever be *done*," Rolf said as they made their way to the front hall. "I mean, there's new rooms every week. And then things get moved around. But it's always going to be that way. You should let Father see it." Rolf snorted. "I know that the new Emissary to Foreign Lands would like a copy. He keeps getting lost. I found him wandering around the passages that lead to the laundry the other day, apparently looking for the council's private study." He shook his head.

"Do you think he's . . . a good person?" Celie had not spent a lot of time with the new Emissary, and since the old Emissary had tried to have her parents killed, she was more than a little uncertain of his replacement.

"Oh, he's fine," Rolf said, offhand. They were in the main hall now.

"I'm going to go to the village and find Pogue," Rolf said. "Coming?"

"I have to change and then help Mother and Lilah," Celie said. "Lilah and I are supposed to get more new gowns. And apparently it's rude to go to a gown fitting in an old gown." She held up her sleeves, which were admittedly too short, but she liked that, as it made it easier to sketch. She saw an ink spot on her cuff and licked it to see if it would go away.

"I don't understand that sort of thing at all," Rolf admitted. "If it has no visible stains and I can lace it up, I'll wear it." He made a face. "I'd better get going, then, or Mother will have me trying on new tunics."

They went their separate ways. Celie found a gown that wasn't too small, or too fancy, and even brushed her hair and found matching stockings. Halfway to the seamstresses' quarters, she remembered the history of Sleyne that she was supposed to be reading for Master Humphries. She would probably spend a great deal of time sitting and waiting on Lilah and her mother, and decided that she might as well get some of the reading done. She made her way to the spiral staircase that led to the schoolroom and went up.

And up. And up. And found herself in the empty corridor once more. She hurried along it, and there was the shallow set of steps that led to the tower. And there in the tower was the egg.

She gingerly put her hand on the shell. It was still very hot, though it didn't burn her this time. When she touched it, it rocked back and forth as though excited. Celie gave the egg a little pat and then backed out of the tower again, heart pounding. She didn't care what Bran said: there *could* be a dragon in an egg that big. And even if it wasn't, if it was a roc, that was still amazing and scary at the same time. She needed to get Bran to look at it. And maybe Lulath. He might have seen a roc's egg before.

"I'll be right back," Celie called toward the egg.

She picked up her skirts and ran to the spiral staircase, wanting to find Bran or even Master Humphries before the tower disappeared again. Halfway down the spiral stairs she found the landing for the schoolroom again and burst out, calling for Master Humphries. He wasn't there, and when she turned around to keep going down to find Bran, she saw with a sinking heart that the spiral stairs didn't go any higher.

“I’m not imagining it,” Celie said, feeling her fingertips, which were still warm. “There is a tower, and there is an egg in it!”

But would she ever find it again? And what was inside the egg?

Chapter 3

Celie found the roofless tower again. In fact, in the following days, she found it nearly every morning, and every time she had a free moment. She had no more than to think of the egg before her feet were carrying her to the spiral staircase and the Castle was leading her upward.

It had been a very cold winter, and another snowstorm had left several inches of snow in the roofless tower, which Celie had swept away with a borrowed broom. She'd also borrowed some heavy horse blankets and an oilcloth from the stables and carefully covered the egg with them.

And so she fell into a pattern. Every morning she'd get up early and hurry to dress and eat breakfast, in order to spend some time with the egg before her lessons. When she got to the tower, she'd shake the frost or sometimes snow off the oilcloth and uncover the egg. It was still always hot, and she would prod it carefully with a gloved hand. It always rocked in reply, and then she would talk to it. She sang to it, too, and even read her lessons to it. She brought up some cushions to sit on and some dried fruits and biscuits to munch while she sat with it.

She thought several times of telling her family, and even tried to lead Rolf up to the tower one day. But whenever someone was with her, the spiral staircase ended just outside the schoolroom. It was as clear as if it had been written on the stones of the Castle itself: the egg was just for her.

Besides which, everyone in the Castle seemed to be very busy. Bran and Pogue were locked in the Armor Gallery every day, making strange noises and occasionally eerie lights and puffs of smoke as they tested the armor and weapons. Rolf had a great many duties, like attending their father, King Glower, at audiences and meetings with the Council. King Glower had insisted on Rolf doing this since the summer before, when their father had been assumed dead and Rolf had briefly become king. And their sister, Lilah, was busy flirting with both the Grathian prince Lulath and Pogue, which was hardly new or unusual, but still very time-consuming for her, and (in Celie's opinion) irritating.

Then late one Wednesday afternoon, the egg hatched.

Celie had been sitting with her back against the blanket-swathed egg, sketching the new stables that had appeared the day before. The egg had rocked, and rocked again, tipping up onto one end so that it knocked most of the blankets off. Celie scrambled to her feet, tossing aside her half-finished map and pencils.

"Don't be a dragon, don't be a dragon," Celie chanted, her fingers and toes crossed.

The egg was rocking so wildly that it was almost standing on end. It was now far too hot for her to touch, despite the light snow that was starting to fall. Celie could see the snowflakes sizzling as they touched the orange shell, which practically glowed in the fading daylight.

"Don't be a dragon," Celie said one last time, as hairline cracks began to appear across the shell.

She was fairly certain it wasn't a dragon, but there was always a small chance. From what information she had been able to glean about creatures that laid very large eggs, it was most likely a roc. Lulath had happily given her a book about them, though it was mostly poetry and legends. It turned out that no one had ever seen a roc egg, but that was because rocs ate horses and, frequently, their riders.

The rocs had almost completely died out in the last century, and Celie had visions of riding to Grath in triumph and delivering the newly hatched baby roc to the mountain caves. A pair of adult rocs would swoop down and bow their proud heads to her before carrying off the baby she had successfully hatched and nursed during its first growth.

The egg stopped rocking.

Celie waited.

After two or three minutes, she became concerned. Surely the beast should have broken free by now? Or at least resumed rocking? She had been reading about the care and training of falcons and other large birds, preparing for the hatching, and knew that it wasn't good to help them out of the shell. If the little creature wasn't strong enough to break free, then it probably wasn't going to live anyway.

That last thought startled a little sob out of Celie's throat. She flung herself down on the mossy nest and started pushing at the cracks in the egg, burning her fingertips but not caring. Suddenly a segment at the very top popped free, like a trapdoor. Celie stood up on her knees and leaned over, closing one eye to peer into the opening.

She fell back with a scream as a golden beak jutted from the hole, nearly jabbing her in the eye.

The egg simply exploded, shards flying everywhere, as Celie cowered, her arms protecting her face. When it was done, she lowered her arms and looked at the wet, crying, and terribly hideous creature in the nest.

"You're not a roc," she said uncertainly.

The creature stumbled toward the sound of her voice, screeching. It tripped over its long lion's tail and fell on its eagle face, wings entangled in its claws.

"What am I going to do with a griffin?" Celie wailed.

Chapter 4

What Celie apparently needed to do with a griffin was feed it, right away. It came at her, sticky and crying, and she scrambled away from it. But it caught a beakful of her gown and started to gnaw on it.

"Stop that!" Celie pulled the gown free.

The griffin let out a wail.

"Here, here!"

Celie pulled out one of the biscuits that she'd brought to snack on and shoved it into the griffin's beak. Then she yanked her hand away quickly as he nearly snapped up her fingers along with the biscuit. The biscuit was gone in a flash, and the griffin wailed and began to search for more. Celie flipped the lid off the entire tin and shoved them under the griffin's questing beak.

It snapped and snaffled and snarled as it ate, flinging crumbs everywhere. Celie couldn't take her eyes off the creature. As its fur and feathers dried, it was taking on a golden hue. The griffin's feet were too big for its body, and so was its round, eagle-like head. But then, most baby animals were ugly and gangly that way. And a griffin was odd to begin with, with its eagle's head, wings, and claws and its back end like a lion's, complete with long tasseled tail.

It was hideous and marvelous at the same time. Wild and fragile, frightening and lovable. Celie put out a hand and ran it over one of the griffin's wings, and it made a cooing noise at her. Her heart gave a little flutter.

After it had eaten all the biscuits, it crawled over to Celie again. Her first instinct was to flee, but she gathered her courage and held out her arms instead. It climbed happily into her lap and began crooning and rubbing its head against her. She was now covered in a nasty, sticky substance that was drying in unpleasant clumps on her skirt, but there was something about the griffin all the same. And the Castle did want her to take care of it, after all. She felt something blooming in her chest as she looked down at the little griffin. She hugged it tighter, and it rubbed its soft head against her arm.

But it was snowing, and Celie knew that she couldn't possibly leave the griffin in the roofless tower all night. She would have to take him back to her bedroom, which was quite a ways away. Celie decided it was best not to think about it too much, and bundled the griffin into her cloak. She heaved her bag of books onto one shoulder, gathered up the writhing bundle, and half ran down the steps and out into the corridor. As she hurried along, the griffin squirming in her arms, she prayed that she wouldn't meet anyone.

At the end of the corridor, just as she was about to start down the stairs, there was a little lurch, and Celie felt a funny twist at the back of her head. She blinked a few times, and when her head cleared a bit she saw that the staircase in front of her had changed. It wasn't the spiral staircase anymore, but a narrow, dark, straight set of stairs with an iron railing set into the stone. With a sigh of relief she realized that this staircase was at the end of the corridor where her bedroom was located.

It was also the corridor where Bran's bedroom was located, so it really shouldn't have surprised her to run straight into her oldest brother as she barreled down the stairs and along the stone-flagged floor. She nearly dropped the griffin, which squawked and tried to climb up her chest in indignation. Bran leaped back in alarm.

"What is that?"

"It's nothing," Celie said, edging around him while she tried to contain the griffin. She didn't dare look down to be sure, but it felt like some of his limbs had come free of the cloak.

"It's not nothing," Bran said severely. "Did you take a puppy from the kennels? You know we're not supposed to do that; those are hunting dogs. They don't make good pets, Celie."

"It's not a dog from the kennels," Celie said, desperately

trying to hold on as the griffin made a frantic sort of lunge. "It's one of Lulath's," she said in a sudden burst of inspiration. "I took her for a walk but she got all muddy, so I'm going to bathe her before I take her back to him."

"Oh," Bran said, relaxing. "I thought I saw them all with him before, but who can tell, he has so many!" He laughed.

Celie tried to force a laugh of her own as she continued to sidle down the corridor. "I know! He has four now, but they seem like a whole herd. I'd better get this one washed."

"Wizard Bran?"

Celie turned with a little shriek. A young page was standing only a pace or so behind her. "Where did you come from?" Celie demanded.

He blushed a deep red. "I—I—Prince Rolf asked me to see if Wizard Bran was coming back to the Armor Gallery."

"Yes, yes, I'm done here," Bran said. He locked the door of his chambers and pocketed the key. He had always been secretive, even as a boy, and if anything it had gotten worse since he'd become a wizard. King Glower said it was because now he had actual secrets to keep.

"What were you doing?" Celie couldn't help but ask, even as she feared that she was losing her grip on the griffin, and her bag was sliding down her shoulder toward her elbow.

"Writing to the College of Wizardry," Bran said. "I need some advice about a few of these exotic weapons, and one of my former tutors there is an expert on magical weaponry."

"Really? Did you send a pigeon?"

Celie was momentarily diverted. Bran had a cage full of white pigeons that he used to send messages to other wizards. Celie loved watching him write codes on tiny scrolls and then seal them into brass tubes that fastened to the pigeons' legs. Usually he invited her to help, and she was put out that he hadn't included her this time.

"I looked for you, Cel, but didn't know where you were," Bran said, seeing her expression.

"What is *that*?" The page was staring at her bundle, which gave another heave.

"Just one of Prince Lulath's dogs," Celie said. She started toward her room again.

"Does he have another?" The page looked vaguely horrified. "He was outside the new gallery with Prince Rolf just now, and he had four with him—four!"

"Oh, good heavens, don't tell me he's gotten a fifth," Bran said, looking at Celie's bundle. "I couldn't bear it."

"No," Celie said innocently. "Just the four. You must have counted wrong," she told the page. "They move around a lot. Like a herd of sheep." She wondered if she should sprint for her room and apologize later. She could feel an exposed claw dangling near her left knee.

"Oh, there were four," the page said, standing square in the middle of the corridor. "He *introduced* them all to me." He sounded even more horrified.

"That's fun," Celie said desperately. "If you'll excuse me, this one is muddy all over and getting heavier by the minute."

"I'll tell Prince Rolf that you are on your way, Lord Wizard," the page said.

He began to back away, and Celie wanted to scream at him to just leave, because she was now in very real danger of dropping the griffin. The page turned at last and left.

She put on her best impression of Lilah and tried to sail gracefully past Bran, but the griffin had other ideas. She had taken no more than a step when it gave one more lurch and freed itself from both the cloak and her arms.

It landed on the floor with its limbs splayed, wings askew, and squalled. Celie dropped to her knees at once, rushing to reassure the little animal and make sure that it wasn't hurt.

"Poor baby," Celie said, soothing it. "Mummy's here, you're all right."

Bran let out a startled yell and then stood over her, his face aghast. "Celie," he said flatly. "That is *not* a dog."

Chapter 5

Oh, Celie, *what have you done?*" Bran asked in a strangled voice.

They had gotten the griffin to Celie's room before anyone else could come along the corridor. There Bran ascertained in quick order that the creature was not hurt, that it was indeed a griffin, and that it was male, and demanded to know once again what Celie had done.

"Why do you say that like this is such a bad thing?" Celie pushed her hair back in exasperation. It was damp with sweat from carrying the griffin, and sheer nerves, and she had lost her ribbon somewhere along the way. "It's not like I purposefully brought a griffin here. I don't even know where griffins come from!"

"That's true, I suppose," Bran said, rubbing his chin. "But you're sure that you didn't ask the Castle for it?"

She stared at him in disbelief. "What would I have said?

Dear Castle, may I please have a griffin egg? And could it hatch on my favorite gown and ruin it?"

"All right," Bran agreed, holding up his hands in a placating gesture. "It was a silly question. But where did you get a baby griffin? And when?"

"He hatched only an hour ago," Celie said.

Then she related the whole story to Bran. A minute into her tale, Bran took out a notebook and began to scribble, his face intent. The griffin began to chew on the rug and whine again, so while she talked, Celie fed him the dried fruit and nuts from her bag, and then the winter apples she had in a bowl by her window.

When she got to the end of her story, where she ran into Bran in the corridor, she found her brother gazing at her in wonder.

"You really hatched a griffin?" Bran asked softly.

"Yes," Celie said, feeling uncomfortable.

"That's amazing, Cel," Bran said. "Truly it is. You managed to care for and hatch an egg—in this weather, no less—and now look at him. He clearly adores you."

The baby griffin was indeed crawling all over Celie, nuzzling her and crying for food.

"He just likes me because I gave him food," Celie said, blushing.

"That's exactly right," Bran said, sounding just a bit jealous. "You fed him first, so he thinks you're his mother."

"He—what?"

The griffin, now that he was dry, was quite a bit larger

than Celie had originally thought. He was roughly twice the size of one of Lulath's lapdogs, and that was without the wings. And as for his wings, they were constantly getting tangled up in his feet or caught on the furniture, and his cries of distress were harsh and loud. Adorable as he was, in an ugly way, she was rather hoping that the Castle would soon send him back to his parents. Taking care of him was going to be quite a chore, even without keeping it secret. She had already sworn Bran to secrecy, knowing that the Castle wouldn't mind him knowing, and having a wizard's help might come in handy.

"Imprinting," Bran said, nodding his head. "A great many animals imprint on the first adult animal they see, or the first that feeds them."

"Oh, dear," Celie said. "I didn't know."

"I'm sure that the Castle did, though," Bran said, thoughtful. "The Castle wanted this griffin to imprint on you."

"But why? Why couldn't the Castle just leave it for its parents to raise?"

Celie tried not to sound frantic. She knew that he would need to eat again, and soon, but she had a feeling that biscuits and raisins weren't going to sustain him forever. And those were all gone anyway.

"Because it doesn't have parents," Bran said. "There's no such thing as a griffin; they're myths. That egg was most likely a fluke: a wizard's experiment from long ago. And who knows how long it has been in that tower, waiting for the Castle to pull it out of . . . wherever the Castle was keeping it."

"Griffins are not just a myth," Celie said hotly. "They come from the Castle. They drove out the unicorns in the third century."

Bran stared at Celie.

"Unicorns?" he asked finally.

"This valley was once the home of a herd of unicorns," Celie said. "Then one day there was an earthquake, and when the shaking stopped, Castle Glower appeared. Griffins came flying out of the Castle and attacked the unicorns. Those that survived fled."

"Where did they go?" Bran had gotten caught up in the story in spite of himself.

"To Larien," she said promptly.

"The Land of a Thousand Waterfalls?" Bran murmured. "Interesting. They say that you can see a rainbow there every day." His fingers twitched and he looked thoughtful; then he started scribbling the story down.

Celie went on. "Supposedly they were taken to Larien on ships that sailed out of Grath, because the Grathian fleet took pity on them. But even Larien was not far enough away, and eventually the unicorns had to seek sanctuary elsewhere."

"Where?"

Celie squirmed a little. "Well, this part is definitely just a myth, but they say that they galloped up a rainbow and into another world. It rains so much there that they really do have rainbows every day. And they're bright, too, and big—you can imagine . . . you can imagine a unicorn running up one."

Celie rather wished she hadn't said anything. It was a fascinating story that she'd found in another book Lulath had given her, and even though it hadn't been about rocs, she'd read it several times because it talked about the Castle.

"Where did you hear this? In one of those romances Lilah is always reading?"

"No," Celie replied quickly. "It was a book Lulath gave me, when I asked him about rocs." Seeing Bran's confusion, she added, "I thought it was a Grathian roc egg."

"Do you still have this book?" Bran asked. "I'm particularly wondering about the part with the Castle. If there's a description of what the valley looked like before, and any indication of how old the myth is and when the event was supposed to have taken place, I would love to see it."

"Er," Celie said. "Sort of. It says something about a flat meadow, and now it's a valley. But when I was done with the book, I forgot and left it in the library. . . . I think it got shelved by accident."

She made a face, and Bran winced in sympathy. The Castle librarian was very old, and very possessive, and sometimes it was hard to make him give up a book once he'd gotten his paws on it.

"I'll have to speak to the librarian about that," Bran said reluctantly. "Or maybe I'll have Pogue look into it," he added, half to himself, as he continued to write in his little notebook.

Celie yelped and snatched her fingers back. The baby griffin had just tried to eat them.

"We need more food for him," Bran told her in an irritatingly knowledgeable way.

"I can't just order the kitchen to send me up a plate of . . . I don't even know what he eats!" Celie fretted. "They'll get suspicious no matter what! I never ask for food in my room, Cook hates that. And he probably needs raw meat or liver or something!"

Celie had been reading a book on falcon keeping, and the author recommended raw organ meats, but also dried corn and flax seeds—all of which were sure to raise Cook's eyebrows and have her asking Queen Celina for an explanation.

"Allow me," Bran said. He stood up and gave her a small bow.

He strode over and tugged the fat-tasseled bellpull in the corner of Celie's room. A few minutes later, a maid knocked on the door. Celie tried to cover the griffin with her body, but Bran blocked the view into the room with his tall form and sweeping robes.

"Ah, hello!" Bran greeted the maid. "I am helping my sister, Princess Cecelia, with an experiment for her lessons.

Could you please go to the kitchens and ask Cook for some raw meat? It doesn't need to be the choice cuts, it can be the organs and fatty bits. Also a bowl of fruit—"

"Dried corn," Celie said in a low, urgent voice.

"And some dried corn."

"Yes, my Lord Wizard," the maid said, and hurried off.

"I wish *I* was the Royal Wizard," Celie grumbled.

"We'll see if we can't get something set up with the kitchens," Bran said. "I'll go and talk to Cook myself."

"What if she says something to Master Humphries?" Celie asked. "What happens if he tells her that I haven't been assigned an experiment involving raw meat and dried corn?"

"Well," Bran began, "perhaps—"

As Celie turned her attention to the griffin, to stop him from gnawing on the leg of a stool, she had an idea.

"I'll ask the Castle," she said. "After all, it wants me to take care of the griffin, so it should provide the food!"

"Do you think it's going to do what you ask?" Bran said, looking skeptical. "It's been very . . . capricious lately."

Her clothes were filthy, and the bites and scratches on her hands were beginning to sting. She had a griffin to take care of, and she didn't know how, and for all Bran's speeches about her being entrusted with the griffin and its imprinting on her, he didn't seem to think she knew how to take care of it, either. She suddenly felt like crying, and she wanted Bran to leave.

"Celie, do you want to get washed up?" Bran, with his wizardly intuition, seemed to guess her mood at once.

"Yes," Celie managed to say without quavering.

"Why don't I hurry the food along, and you and the griffin can freshen up. We'll just deal with this one day at a time."

"Oh!" As Celie stood up, her stomach growled audibly, to her embarrassment. "Is it dinnertime?"

"Yes," Bran said, looking vague. "I think we'd better . . . Hmm." He tapped his lower lip. "I'll go on to the dining hall and tell them that you're working on a project for Master Humphries and can't join us," Bran said. "I'll have a tray sent up for you, and I'll come check on you after dinner."

"Perfect," Celie said. "Thanks, Bran."

She didn't burst into exhausted tears until after she had latched the door behind him.

Chapter 6

Celie spent the next week watching the little griffin eat and grow.

The Castle went out of its way to support her in this, and to make sure that the griffin was well provided for. Every morning when Celie woke up, with a warm, sleepy griffin curled against her side, she found fresh sawdust in a box in the corner, a large urn of water, and bowls of fresh meat, seeds, and fruit. There was even a leather ball for him to play with.

Celie had been worried about the maids finding the griffin, but Bran put a spell on her door the very first night that made them turn away, thinking that they'd already cleaned Celie's chamber. She asked him to put a spell on everyone in the Castle so that they couldn't see the griffin—which she had named Rufus—but Bran had frowned at her.

"There is a very great difference between bespelling

your door and bespelling a person," Bran said, bristling at her. "The Council of Wizards would have my head if they thought I was even contemplating such a thing."

At the end of the first week, the griffin had nearly doubled in size, and his cries had become three times as shrill. Celie had a hard time keeping him entertained: most of her furniture was scraped and chewed, and her new riding boots were ruined. Bran came to her rooms to measure and sketch the griffin, and she asked him again to use magic to make the animal less noticeable, at least.

"I don't see why you won't just tell Father," Bran replied. "I promised you I wouldn't, but that's because I think you should be the one to do it. Really, Celie, there's only so long you'll be able to hide him."

"I know, but I don't know what else to do," she said. "I actually tried to tell Mummy and Daddy at breakfast the very next morning. I was so exhausted; he kept me up all night whining and begging for food. But as soon as I opened my mouth to do it, that pack of cloaks fell down the chimney."

"Oh, that," Bran said.

The family had been at breakfast in the winter dining hall, and Celie had just gotten her parents' attention when a sooty bundle had fallen down the chimney into the fireplace with a startling thump. Rolf had hurried to pull it out of the fire with the iron tongs, and they had discovered that it was a bundle of oddly shaped old cloaks that had probably been shoved up the chimney centuries before.

The cloaks were shaped like oak leaves, and made from leather that had been washed and pounded until it was as soft as the finest wool. In the ensuing excitement, Celie had lost her opportunity to tell her parents.

"And I almost told them the next day," she said, "when I got back from my lessons and found that he'd eaten my new boots. But as soon as I decided to, the door of my room locked itself. I couldn't get out until I promised that I wouldn't tell anyone about Rufus."

"Rufus?" Bran raised his eyebrows.

"I named him Rufus," Celie said, defensive. "It's a good name for a griffin."

Rufus had been the name of the stuffed lion she had had since she was a baby. Last year, during the old Emissary's attempt to get rid of their family and put Prince Khelsh of Vhervhine on the throne, Rufus the lion had turned into a griffin—and eaten Prince Khelsh. Then he had simply disappeared. The baby griffin was considerably smaller than Rufus the Stuffed-Lion Griffin, but Celie still thought it was a very good name for a griffin.

"Oh," Bran said. "I, er, brought a list of names you might like. But if you've already named him . . ."

"Yes, and he answers to it," Celie said with pride. She picked up the leather ball. "Rufus!" The griffin immediately looked up from the bone it was chewing. "Fetch!" She tossed the ball, and the little beast ran across the room after it. Celie turned back to her oldest brother. "Why? What names did you think of?"

"Oh, nothing," Bran said.

Looking up at him, Celie saw that her tall, commanding brother—the Royal Wizard, no less—was blushing. He shoved a scrap of parchment into his pocket.

"What were the names?" Celie was intrigued.

"They were silly," Bran said. "Anyway, if the Castle is locking you in your room, and possibly even dropping things down the chimney, then it definitely wants you to keep Rufus a secret." He sighed. "Even though I think it's a rather strange idea, having to keep a wild animal in your bedcham—Hey!"

Celie had sidled around Bran and grabbed the slip of parchment from his pocket. "Goldenwings . . ." She looked at the names in incredulity. Bran? Pragmatic, studious *Bran* had written down *Goldenwings* as a potential name for her griffin? "Proudheart. Proudwings. Brightclaw."

"Give that back!" Bran snatched the list away, his face bright red.

"I'm not laughing at you," she said, contrite when she saw how hurt he was. "I'm just laughing because . . . Well, *Proudwings*?"

"I was looking for a noble name," he said stiffly. "Something that evoked the steeds of the great heroes of legend."

Now Celie really did feel bad. "Those are very noble names," she offered. "But I'm not sure that a creature who can't stop eating my shoes deserves to be called something like Brightclaw." And with a sigh she went to pull one of her dancing slippers out of Rufus's beak.

"True," Bran said, looking mollified. "I had better get to the Armor Gallery," he said with a sigh. "Still more to study there."

"I should think you'd be more excited," Celie said, tossing the ball for Rufus to distract him from her shoes. "All those strange bits of armor and weaponry . . ."

"Yes, they're all very well," Bran said. "But you know that all my life I've wanted to uncover the secrets of the Castle itself, and not just one of the rooms." His shoulders slumped. "Besides which, most of the things aren't from the Castle, they're from some other land. It's just adding mystery to mystery. I'll never figure out where most of the artifacts came from, let alone what they're for. And when I'm finally done with them, I'll be further than ever from finding out about Castle Glower." He ran a hand over his face. "You've done more to unlock the Castle's mysteries with your atlas than anyone living, yet I'm the one who spent years learning to be a wizard!"

"Oh, dear," Celie said. Her eyes flicked to her desk.

"What's that?" Bran followed her gaze. "Is it finished?" He picked up the atlas on the top of the neat stack.

"Yes," Celie told him reluctantly. "I was going to pass out copies at dinner. But now I don't want to . . . to show you up."

She had declared the atlas finished a few days previous, and had given it to the Castle scribes. They had made four copies and put them in leather folders. She had planned to give one to her parents and the others to Bran, Rolf, and

Lilah at dinner, but she worried now that it would make Bran look bad.

Bran must have immediately sensed her regret. He turned to her with a broad smile.

"This is truly amazing, Cel. No one has ever done anything like this!" He reverently turned the pages of maps. "Could I have one of the copies?"

"Of course!" She made a pushing motion at him, indicating that he should keep the atlas in his hands.

"This is really something special, Celie," Bran said. "Can I have another copy made? One of my tutors from the College of Wizardry, Wizard Levin, is coming to stay here and help me with the Armor Gallery."

"He is?" Celie was startled and excited by this piece of news. Other than Bran, she'd rarely seen any real wizards before.

"Yes," Bran said. "And he'll need a copy so that he can get around. And hopefully with him here, I will have more time to study the Castle and spend less time hunched over meaningless artifacts."

"I wish I could help," Celie said.

Now that she was done with her atlas—at least until the Castle produced a new room, and then it would only take her a day to sketch it and have copies made—she was feeling a bit let down. True, there was Rufus to care for, but she had been working on the atlas for so long, it felt strange to be done.

"I could use your help," Bran admitted.

"How? Why?" Distracted, Celie let Rufus nip at her fingers and gown as she gave her full attention to Bran.

"I want you to find out what connection there is between griffins and the Castle," Bran said. "Find that book you left in the library, see if you can't find more references to griffins appearing at the Castle." Bran held up one of the maps to study it better. "Where did that egg come from, and why did the Castle give it to you, specifically?"

"Excellent," Celie said eagerly. "I think I'll start by sketching the tapestries."

"What tapestries?" Bran looked up, confused.

"The ones in the upper corridors," Celie said. "You know: the ones that show our ancestors riding griffins into battle."

Chapter 7

The presentation of the remainder of the atlases at dinner was everything Celie had hoped for. Her family praised her greatly, and her father spoke of giving her a special title—Royal Cartographer to the Castle—which she was sure made her face turn positively mauve. Back in her room, she'd told Rufus all about it while he gazed at her with golden eyes and lovingly chewed the hem of her gown.

But the next morning, several of her maps were rendered useless. There was another new stable, which had demolished part of the outer wall and let a number of cows into the courtyard. And Celie was late for her lessons because there was now an extra portrait gallery and a large storeroom containing hundreds of bolts of fabric between her and the schoolroom.

Then, when she finally got to the schoolroom, Lilah and Rolf were both there. Celie took a step back and looked around, wondering what they were doing there. Had they gotten lost on their way to someplace else in the Castle? Lilah looked distinctly put out, but Rolf seemed eager enough. He waved cheerfully to Celie and stretched, resting his hands behind his head. Celie put down her books on the end of the long table, still feeling muddled by her roundabout journey to the schoolroom.

"What are you doing here?" Celie asked, her voice coming out a little harsh as she looked at her brother and sister.

"*I* am learning Grathian because it will help me be a better king," Rolf said easily. "But Lilah is learning Grathian because she's being punished." He grinned at Celie.

Lilah slammed closed the book she was holding. "I am not being *punished*!" She tossed back her long, dark hair. "It is also important that I study the languages of some of our allies, even though I am too old for the schoolroom," she said in lofty tones.

"Father caught her flirting with Lulath one too many times," Rolf said in a stage whisper. "So he's pretending that he believes her story that she was really trying to learn Grathian."

"But what about Pogue?" Celie asked Lilah.

"What *about* Pogue?" Lilah threw her hands in the air. "Can't I just have friends? Can't I enjoy talking to my . . . friends?"

"There's talking, and then there's *talking*," Rolf said with a snicker.

"And then there's listening to your instructor," Master Humphries said as he entered the schoolroom.

He shook his head, running an ink-stained hand through his graying hair. When he looked at the three of them sitting in a row he let out a puff of air. Celie had a feeling that he wasn't amused to find that he now had two more students, and one of them sent there as punishment.

"I'm sorry I'm late, Master," Celie said. "There's a huge room full—"

"Of fabrics," Master Humphries finished. "Yes, thank you, Your Highness. I am late myself for that very reason. And so is your new Grathian instructor."

All three Glower children looked at their tutor in shock. Master Humphries had taught all their lessons since he had come to the Castle to instruct the then five-year-old Bran. If they needed to learn something that he did not already know, he took great pains to master the topic himself before guiding his charges through it. He was overly fascinated by ancient peace treaties (in Celie's opinion) and could be a bear about punctuality, but was a respected scholar and a fine tutor.

"Your instructor in Grathian will be—" Master Humphries began.

"I am all the excitement," Prince Lulath shouted as he practically leaped into the schoolroom. "Please to forgive that I so the very late; there is but a great many makings of clothes now in the place where there was used to having a stairs."

"I want to die," Lilah said in a strangled voice.

"This is going to be terrific," Rolf said under his breath.

"Lulath!" Celie cried in delight. "*You're* going to teach us?"

Celie stared at the Grathian prince. He had all four dogs in tow, the satin bows around their necks matching his elaborate layers of clothing. His sleeves hung to his knees, and one of his dogs became entangled in the trailing ends of the laces that ran up the sides of his breeches. His blond hair was fancifully styled, and his teeth showed very white as he beamed at them.

"Yes, indeed, Your Highness," Master Humphries answered her, forcing a smile. "As my Grathian is limited to reading and writing, Prince Lulath has nobly agreed to teach you how to speak it. It was the suggestion of the king himself."

Rolf snorted.

Lulath's dogs scattered. One of them trotted around the room, sniffing everything as if seeking a place to relieve itself. Two others, JouJou and Niro, ran to Celie and Lilah, who were their favorite people. Lilah hid her blushing cheeks by leaning over to pick up Niro, but Celie just rolled JouJou over with her feet and rubbed the dog's belly with her toes.

"I have given each of the students a Grathian language primer," Master Humphries said in a desperate attempt to bring things to order. "If you're having trouble getting started, I'm sure that I can—"

"It would be so much nonsense to think I could not tell

to them my language," Lulath said exuberantly. "Come, let us speak to each one another in the Grathian!" He held his arms out wide as if to embrace them all, and smiled in his usual faintly daft way. Then, so abrupt that it was startling, his expression sobered. He picked up another primer and announced crisply, "We begin with *minou*."

And to the utter shock of Celie, Rolf, Lilah, and Master Humphries, Lulath began to teach them with cool competence. He ignored his dogs and his students' complete amazement as he took them through the basic greetings and then taught them how to introduce themselves in Grathian.

Two hours later, when a maid came bearing a lunch tray, they were still stunned. Lulath instantly became a dandy once again, and after turning up his nose at the ham sandwiches on the tray, he gathered up his dogs and left, promising to return the next day and teach them more.

Rolf and Lilah left after lunch, and Celie and Master Humphries were soon hard at work. She was supposed to be practicing her calligraphy by copying out a poem from a book so old it was nearly unreadable. It had been Master Humphries's choice, and his taste in poetry always ran toward the epic, with lots of names and battles mentioned, but not described in half as much detail as Celie would have liked. Consequently, she was halfway through it when she found the word "griffin" and realized that the poem was about a mighty battle between the griffins and an army that Celie had never heard of.

"What are Hathelockes?" Celie asked.

Master Humphries, who was flipping through a book and seemed to have forgotten that Celie was there, nearly dropped what he was reading. He blinked at her owlishly.

"The what?"

"Hathelockes," Celie repeated. "It says that the griffins and the people of the griffins were making war upon the Hathelockes. I've never heard of them."

"Oh, er," Master Humphries began, attempting to read the faded poem upside down. "This is an old and rather fanciful poem," he told her. "Notice the presence of mythical animals in it? I'm sure that the Hathelockes are also merely the construction of the poet's mind."

"But the griffins might be real," Celie protested.

"My dear princess, they most certainly are not."

Celie gave up, but she carefully copied the rest of the poem and took it with her. She wanted to read it aloud to Rufus, to teach him about his noble heritage. She also wanted to show it to Bran. She tried to take the book as well, but Master Humphries had taken it from the oldest section of the Castle library and promised to return it directly after lessons. Celie had to make do with copying down the title and author of the book, and hoping that Bran would be able to find it himself.

She made the long journey back to her bedroom, wondering if the Castle would send her a snack as well as Rufus.

"Rufus," she called as she opened her bedroom door. "Rufus! I have something to read to you!"

There was no answer. Rufus was gone.

Chapter 8

Celie looked in the wardrobe and under the bed, but she knew that Rufus wasn't there. He would have come when she called if he could hear her, he always did. She tossed the parchment with the poem on it onto her bed and hurried back out of the room.

A quick glance told her that he wasn't in the main hall. There were members of the court milling around there as usual, and guards posted at the front door. Someone would have seen Rufus as soon as he set a foot in that direction, and the resulting hue and cry would have brought the entire Castle running.

Instead she raced down the corridor in the opposite direction. At the end of the corridor was a long flight of steps, the same one that she had come down to bring the newly hatched Rufus to her bedchambers. The steps were steep and narrow, the stone slick. She didn't think Rufus could have made it up them, not without being seen by a maid or a courtier.

Celie walked back along the corridor, heart racing. She tried listening at Bran's door, but her breathing was too loud for her to hear through the heavy oak. Bran always locked his door anyway, and Rufus couldn't undo a lock. With a sick feeling, she remembered pulling her own door closed, but not locking it when she left for her lessons that morning. Since Bran had put the spell on her door, she had been overconfident that no one would go in. She had never thought that Rufus would find a way to get out.

Her heart pounding even harder, she went across the corridor to Lilah's door. She turned the latch and it opened; Lilah never locked her door. Celie stepped inside, holding her breath.

Lilah's room was beautiful: everything neatly in place, furniture gleaming with polish, and pillows plumped. Lilah had hung long silk scarves and sashes from a rack in the corner like a captive rainbow, and the windows were thrown open to show the stunning view of a landscape that did not exist. It was like a living painting that the Castle had provided just for Lilah.

Celie let out her breath. "Rufus?" she called softly.

Lilah's room was empty. Celie's heart calmed down, and she started to turn away. Then something gold on the floor caught her eye. She thought at first that it was a belt or sash that had fallen off the bed; then it moved, and she realized that it was Rufus's tail. She hurried around the side of the bed and found him crouched over one of Lilah's brand-new dancing slippers, gnawing away.

"Bad boy! Bad boy! Drop it!"

Celie shook her finger at him, and saw a look of distinct guilt in the griffin's eyes. Even so, she had to pull the mangled slipper out of his beak. It was in pieces, the beads hanging by threads or scattered over the floor, the silk lining in shreds, and the leather scored and torn.

"No, no, no," she scolded him in a whisper. "If Lilah asks, we think Niro did it," Celie told him conspiratorially. She felt guilty, but she could hardly confess to Lilah and take the blame herself. After all, she wasn't prone to eating people's shoes, and Lilah would never believe her. "Now, come on!"

When Rufus seemed reluctant to follow, Celie grabbed hold of his long tail and threatened to haul him backward.

His tail was very long and dragged on the ground, looking almost like it had been tacked on. Bran said this was evidence that Rufus still had a great deal of growing to do, especially since his paws were also enormous when compared to his lanky body. He was now as tall as Celie's hip and weighed almost as much as she did, but he still moved like he wasn't sure how to coordinate his four legs, and his wings were constantly getting caught on things.

Getting Rufus back to Celie's room was not going to be easy.

Celie peeked out of Lilah's door with Rufus hidden behind her skirts, then closed the door quickly as a maid went by. Once she had counted to twenty, she opened the door and looked again. The corridor was empty. Celie got a firm grip on Rufus's tail and dragged him out of Lilah's room. She shut the door so quickly that she nearly closed it on Rufus's rump, and then she hustled him down the corridor.

She reached the door to her own room just as she heard heavy footsteps and men's voices coming from the main hall. She shoved Rufus inside, leaping in after him and slamming the door. Sweat was sticking her curly hair to her forehead.

"You are a very bad griffin," she told him again, panting.

Someone knocked on her door, and Celie let out a small scream and nearly fell over Rufus. She managed to get a grip on herself and bundled Rufus into her water closet before answering the knock, still panting and sweating but without a griffin scrabbling at her skirts.

"Celie!" Queen Celina was clearly startled by her youngest child's appearance. "Are you all right?"

"I just . . . the Castle changed and I couldn't get to the schoolroom . . . and then on my way back . . . I had to use the water closet . . ."

"Oh, I see," Queen Celina said, her expression clearing. "Well, if you're . . . freshened up . . . after your lessons, I want you to come with me."

Celie could hear a scrabbling sound coming from her water closet.

"Why?" She edged toward the door of her room, hoping to press her mother back into the corridor as casually as she could. "Is something the matter?" she asked in a loud voice, to try to cover Rufus's noise.

"Not at all, but you've seen the room full of fabrics?" The queen was smiling now and didn't even wait for Celie's nod. "Of course you have: you had to go through it to get to the schoolroom! Well, Bran has looked it all over and said that it's quite safe. I've called in the seamstresses, and we'll have our new gowns made from these goods. Some of the things are spoiled, but most of it is still in perfect condition, and there are some lovely silks."

"Oh, yes, let's go, then," Celie said loudly. She continued to back her mother out of the room as a loud scrabbling noise came from the water closet.

"What was that?"

"I didn't hear anything," Celie said. She sidled around her mother and grabbed the door latch. "Shall we?"

"Oh, yes," the queen said, though she did throw a puzzled look at Celie's water-closet door. "Perhaps someone ought to—"

"I think that noise is coming from the corridor," Celie said. "Must have been one of the maids passing by."

She heaved a sigh of relief when her mother finally came out of her room. Celie made a pretense of having her sleeve catch on the latch in order to lock her door without her mother noticing. Feeling sweat still trickling down her back, she turned around to follow the queen and let out another little scream. Lilah was standing directly in front of her, holding out a ruined dancing slipper.

"When I find out who—or what—did this, I will make new slippers out of their hide," Lilah said in a dangerous voice.

Chapter 9

When the holiday feasting hall appeared, Celie began to worry about the Castle.

Normally it appeared during the winter holidays, coming into being at sunset and disappearing again at dawn. They would feast and sing and dance among beautiful decorations that were provided and changed every year, and then the Castle would take it all back. But the Tuesday after the roomful of fabric had appeared, the arch into the holiday dining hall stretched open and stayed that way.

Since the king was hearing petitions and Ma'am Housekeeper was on the far side of the Castle overseeing the counting and sorting of some linens, a maid showed up at Celie's door to ask for help. None of the maids wanted to set foot in the holiday feasting hall for fear it would disappear again with them inside it, she explained, and they wanted someone that the Castle respected to have a look.

"I'll come right away," Celie said loudly.

She hurried out of her room, pushing the maid ahead of her, and locked the door. When the maid had knocked, Celie had shoved Rufus under her bed, and she could hear him squawking and trying to work his way out from beneath the trailing bedclothes. She was a little annoyed that the spell Bran had put on her door hadn't worked on the maid, or on her mother a few days before, and now she worried that the spell only worked on maids coming to clean.

When she got to the archway that led to the holiday dining hall, however, she did stop to feel flattered for a moment. There were several maids gathered there, and they all brightened when they saw Celie coming. One of them nodded as though to say that Celie was just the right person to take care of things.

"Has my father been told?" she asked, though she guessed the answer.

"No, Your Highness," the maid who had fetched her said. "We didn't want to disturb him during court."

"If someone would please fetch the Royal Wizard," Celie said.

"Wizard's in the Armor Gallery, Highness," one of the maids said. "And we en't supposed to bother him, either. 'Specially when he's lookin' at them things."

Celie pursed her lips. She pointed to the maid who had come to her room. "Go into the throne room and signal to Prince Rolf. He can leave the petitions easily, and if there's need for my father to come, he can get him."

The girl nodded and hurried across the main hall to the double doors of the throne room. Celie steeled herself to step through the archway, hoping, as the maids had, that it wouldn't whisk her away somewhere.

She could of course see into the room, which looked musty and disused. The long feasting table was shoved against one wall, and there were a number of large crates in the middle of the room. It had never occurred to her before, but there were no windows, and naturally there were no candles lit inside. The room was cavernous and gloomy, and there was dust on everything, even though it was barely two months past the holidays.

The maids were all watching her anxiously. Celie straightened her spine. The Castle had never removed a room with someone in it; it certainly would not start with her. Not while she was raising Rufus for it. She took a step forward.

"What in the name of— Isn't that the holiday feasting hall?"

Pogue Parry's voice carried across the main hall.

"Cel! What are you doing?" Rolf chimed in a moment later.

Celie turned and saw her brother coming out of the throne room with the maid in tow, and Pogue hurrying across the stone floor, hair windblown and cheeks ruddy from being outside.

"Today's new room is the holiday feasting hall," Celie said, feeling strangely relieved. "But it's all gloomy and boxed up. I was just going inside to see what is in those crates."

"Excellent, and very strange," Rolf said. He took her arm. "Let's go together, shall we?" He looked at the maids, his eyes glinting. "Anyone else coming?"

"I'm coming," Pogue said. He put a large hand on Celie's shoulder. "No one else needs to come," Pogue said quietly to the maid hovering nearby.

The three of them took deep breaths and then stepped through the archway together. They stopped just inside the feasting hall. Nothing happened.

"It's safe," Rolf said sharply over his shoulder to the maids.

"Don't be rude," Celie whispered.

"I am not pleased that they got you to take the risk for them," he retorted. "You're not to be the official Castle poison taster, as it were."

"It's fine," Celie said. She slipped out of Rolf and Pogue's grip and went to the first of the crates. Pogue followed, and together they got the lid off. Inside, nestled in straw, were the golden baubles that had hung from the ceiling at the winter feasts. In another crate they found silk streamers carefully wound around spools, and so on. Each crate contained a treasure trove of beautiful things that had been used to make the holiday feasting hall appear magical. But now, packed away like this, they all seemed tawdry and faded.

"Why is this happening?" Celie wanted to know.

"You know what I want to know?" Rolf asked in a hushed voice. The other two looked at him. "I want to know who it is that puts up these decorations every year, then takes them down and packs them away."

Celie looked at him blankly. "The Castle does it," she said finally.

"The Castle would just leave it all up, wouldn't it?" Rolf argued. "It's people who would bother to pack all these things in straw."

A weird, queasy feeling was growing in Celie's middle. She thought about the dusty rooms, the faded tapestries. She'd always thought that the new rooms came to entertain the Glower family and the other people who lived in the Castle. When the holiday feasting hall wasn't in Sleyne, where was it? Were there people feasting on the golden plates every other day of the year? She looked at the crates and the stacked chairs with growing horror.

"What has happened?" Bran swept into the room, looking even more wizardly than usual in formal robes and a round hat. He stopped short. "It's the holiday feasting hall," he said in a hushed voice. He locked gazes with Pogue. "This isn't good," he said.

The sick feeling in Celie's middle grew even worse. What was happening to her Castle?

Chapter 10

How serious is it?" King Glower asked.

The family, plus Lulath and Pogue, were sitting around the table in the winter dining hall. They'd just finished dinner, and Bran had asked to address them all. Celie had hurriedly sketched the newest changes to the Castle and had copies made that afternoon, which she was passing around.

"Well," Bran hedged. "There are a lot of factors to consider, and we're still gathering information."

He tried to put on his mysterious wizard voice to make it seem like he wasn't concerned, but none of the family was fooled. That was the trouble with being both the Royal Wizard and a member of the Glower family, Celie thought.

Bran continued. "But the truth of the matter is . . . we just don't know."

Everyone blinked at him.

Celie, who was just behind Pogue, stopped in her tracks. Pogue froze, too, with his hand up for the map she was giving him. After a moment she remembered herself and gave him the parchment before hurrying to take her place beside Rolf once more.

"What has surprised me since I was old enough to care," Bran continued, "is that in all the years the Castle has been sitting in this valley, almost nothing has been written about it.

"We know the original name of every King Glower, but little to nothing about their lives, and certainly nothing about their dealings with the Castle, other than legends and rumors. There are no maps of the Castle but Celie's, no record of the rooms that have come and gone. The only clues are small mentions here and there in journals or histories, notes about having lunch in the new solar, or holding court in the round tower, that seem to indicate there are rooms that are no longer here."

"We've all seen rooms come and go," King Glower said, but the uneasiness in his voice belied his casual words. "It's the nature of the Castle."

"Of course," Bran said. "But what worries me, other than the lack of information on the Castle—which is strange enough—is that in the last few months the nature of the Castle has changed. We can't vouch for the Castle's behavior prior to, say, fifty years ago, but we can say that within those fifty years, this is the longest the Castle has gone without removing a room."

"How long has it been?" Queen Celina asked, frowning. She tapped her fingers on the table as if counting.

"Two months," Celie said.

Bran nodded. "The last rooms to disappear were the guest rooms used for the winter holidays," he reported. "According to Ma'am Housekeeper, the guest rooms used by Uncle Rupert and Aunt Zelda disappeared the morning after they left for Sleyne City. The maids cleaned them the evening before, put dust covers on the furniture, and the next morning they were gone. Just like they always are."

Celie knew that she couldn't tell them about the hatching tower, which came and went depending on whether she was alone, but she raised her hand as she slid back into her seat. When everyone looked at her, she pointed out that the nursery was gone.

"Actually," Bran said, "it's still here. It's behind the schoolroom; it's just hard to get to."

Celie made a face. She hadn't known that.

"For several months after the unpleasantness last summer with Prince Khelsh," Queen Celina said, "I noticed that the Castle was a great deal more responsive. But that seems to have changed again." Her brows drew together in a frown.

"It's true," King Glower said. "I definitely felt that it was listening to me. It moved things around when Ma'am Housekeeper or I asked. But not only are the odd little rooms and corridors building up, but they seem to be much more . . . inconvenient than before."

"That room full of fabric isn't inconvenient," Lilah interrupted. "It's *fantastic*."

"But it's essentially bisecting the Castle," Pogue argued. "And from the way it's situated, I'm expecting two more rooms and possibly another corridor to join it, making what's now the central part of the Castle into two distinct sections."

Everyone looked at Pogue in surprise, and his brown cheeks turned pink. Lilah gave him a skeptical look, but the king's expression was thoughtful.

"I've been helping Bran," Pogue muttered.

"He's been invaluable," Bran said, shuffling through some notes. "He remembers everything. And from the way that sewing room is situated, and the way the corridor shifted around it, he's right." Bran made some marks on one of Celie's maps with a charcoal pencil and held it up to show them where they could expect the new rooms. "Pogue thinks they'll be here and here, and I agree."

Pogue turned even pinker under his tan.

"And you've looked in my father's journals?" Queen Celina asked. Her father had been the Royal Wizard before Bran. She looked from Bran to Pogue, as though she valued both their opinions equally, to Celie's surprise.

"Many times. He comes the closest to recording the Castle's history," Bran said. "That's why I say we can go back fifty years: Grandfather's journal is our main source of information. But even so, he only makes casual mention of new rooms, though he does note the date." He made a face. "But I still find it very strange that a wizard, living in this Castle, didn't think to make clearer notes."

Celie blurted out what had been worrying her about the holiday feasting hall.

"Are there other people living in the other rooms of the Castle? What do they do when the Castle gives those rooms to us?" she asked. She could tell by the shock on her father's face that he had never considered this before.

Bran nodded, but not to say yes: more to say that her question was a good one. "The extra kitchen, the extra stables, and the sewing room haven't been touched in years. So far as we know, none of these things have appeared in the last fifty years. Which would indicate that there aren't other people living in them, worrying about where their kitchen or feasting hall has gone."

Celie relaxed slightly. A more pressing question rose in her mind: If there weren't people living there, then who put away the decorations? And who had they all belonged to to begin with? But before she could ask, Lilah spoke.

"The fabric hasn't been touched in at least two hundred years," she put in.

"It hasn't? How can you tell?"

Lilah shrugged. "There were sketches for new gowns on the table, covered in dust. The fashions were at least two hundred years old. Though it's odd that the only fabric that got spoiled was that stored by the open window."

"How is that odd?" Bran had his pencil poised above his notebook.

"Fabric rots," Queen Celina answered him. "It gets faded or worn or . . . well, rotten, even if it isn't being worn. But that is in the nature of the Castle, as you know. Sometimes there's even food on the tables, but it's not moldy, just dried out and dusty. That fabric could very well be five hundred years old, but it's still usable. Anywhere else in the world it wouldn't be."

"Interesting." Bran hastily wrote that in his notes. "I may have to do more tests on it."

"Don't you dare," Lilah warned. "You said the fabric wasn't enchanted, and I'm having several gowns made out of it right now. If you ruin any of my new gowns, Bran, then so help me—" She shook a finger at him.

"But we are having the answer to it all right here!" Lulath patted the table lightly and beamed. Everyone turned abruptly to stare at him. "Why are we not asking the Celie to ask the Castle what it means?" He looked at Celie eagerly. "It will surely be having the telling of her!"

Now everyone was looking expectantly at Celie, who stared back. Did they really think the Castle could talk to her? Judging by their expressions, they did.

"I, er, I don't always know what it wants," Celie began, feeling the color rise in her own cheeks.

"Of course not, darling," Queen Celina said. "But perhaps there's some way you could talk to it?"

King Glower was nodding. "There must be some way it could signal to you what it wants," he said. "We must think of something; this is all becoming extremely odd. The fabric might have been a lovely gift from the Castle, but the holiday feasting hall? There's no reason for that to be here now, is there? And empty linen closets serve no purpose, nor does the extra kitchen or the new stables! The stalls aren't even a good size for horses. I don't know what they used to keep in there . . . large goats, maybe?"

"I, er, haven't looked at them," Celie said, feeling a little sweat bead on her upper lip.

"Don't let it worry you, dear," Queen Celina said. "It's not your job to interpret everything the Castle does! We'll figure something out."

But before they could, Ma'am Housekeeper came to the door and cleared her throat. The king stood and waved her in, inviting her to sit down.

"No, Your Majesty, I'm afraid there's quite a to-do in the bedrooms," she said, looking sour. "The maids doing the turndown tonight claim there's a wild animal loose in the Castle. Most likely it's another case of the sheep getting in, but—"

Bran and Celie were already past the housekeeper and headed down the corridor toward the family's bedchambers, which the Castle had conveniently put in a row.

Barely five minutes later Celie and Bran were standing in Bran's rooms, surveying the wreckage of his private study. They'd found Rufus before anyone else saw him, but they'd also found the horrible mess he'd made. A mess that, unfortunately, extended all the way down the corridor.

"How did he even get in my rooms?" Bran wanted to know. "The door was locked—it's always locked!"

Like the other rooms they had passed, Bran's was covered in feathers from shredded pillows. Occasional tables had been overturned, books lay on the floor with covers chewed and pages ripped out, and the leg of Bran's large worktable had been thoroughly gnawed.

Rufus was in the corner, looking subdued but not at all contrite. He was utterly filthy, his fur and feathers ruffled, pillow feathers stuck to him with clumps of what looked like Lilah's expensive Grathian hair pomade. He'd gotten into some of Bran's potions as well, and there was something blue and gooey all down his one side.

"That won't hurt him, will it?" Celie pointed to the blue goo.

"No, but it was expensive." Bran sighed. "You little brat," he said to Rufus. "How *did* you get in here?"

"Do you think the Castle let him in?" Celie looked around. There was no other way but the door, and that, as Bran said, had been locked.

"Why?" The single word held all Bran's frustration and irritation.

"Maybe to protect him?" Celie shrugged. "So that he wouldn't be discovered by Lilah or one of the maids?"

"If *all* of my orchid tears are gone, he'll need to be protected from *me*," Bran said.

Bran's jaw was jutting out, and Celie half believed him. She went over to Rufus and tried to pull him away from the bottles on the floor, wondering if there was some way to have a collar made without specifying what type of animal it was for, when she heard voices in the corridor. She started to throw her hands up in despair at getting Rufus to her room undetected, but she stopped herself, not wanting to lose her tenuous grip on the matted and sticky fur of his shoulders.

"This is ridiculous," Bran said, surveying the mess of his room. "I'm sorry, Celie, but I'm going to tell Father." They could hear their father in the corridor, calling out orders to the servants. "Hiding Rufus is just going to get more complicated, and it honestly makes no sense."

"All right," Celie agreed in a small voice. "I'll tell him. If I can."

"I'll support you," Bran said, putting a hand on her shoulder. "If both of us insist on telling him . . ." Bran trailed off.

Celie felt a funny twist in her head. They turned to the door, Celie still trying to get Rufus under control. But the door had no latch. It had no hinges. It was a solid construction of wood, bound with iron, that blended seamlessly into the stone wall and was completely without a way of being opened.

"Are you joking?" Bran took his hand off Celie's shoulder to rub his face in frustration.

"There's clearly some reason the Castle wants us to keep Rufus a secret," Celie said. "I mean, I'd love to let Mummy and Daddy take over, and not have to worry about him all alone in my room, chewing up my shoes every day. But this happens whenever I think about telling someone."

She gave a little hiccup. She had wondered if she was just imagining that the Castle wanted her to keep Rufus secret because she didn't want him to be taken away from her, but here was proof. She felt a twinge of relief: Rufus was still all hers.

"I don't understand," Bran said slowly. "What does the Castle have to lose if Rufus is seen by our parents? Mother has a great deal of experience with magic, and both she and Father are supporters of all the Castle does . . . of course."

Rufus shook himself, and blue goo and feathers went flying. Bran's mouth tightened into a line. They could still hear their father and others in the corridor, calling out instructions and searching for whatever had done all the damage to the bedrooms.

Celie's mouth also settled into a straight line. She marched over to the wall beside the door and laid one hand on the stones with a flourish.

"What are you—" Bran began.

"Shh!" Celie silenced him. She held up one finger on her free hand. "Listen."

"I am!" Bran said.

"Not you! I'm talking to the Castle," Celie explained. She closed her eyes and tried to ignore her oldest brother.

"I'm trying to take care of Rufus, really I am," she told the Castle, making her voice firm. "And I'm trying to be mindful of your wishes and not tell anyone but Bran about him. But you have got to work with me. I need help. If I don't get it from you, then I will climb out this window and get it from my parents. *Do you understand?*"

Celie was engulfed in a whirlwind. There was a funny twist in her head again. It seemed familiar, but she couldn't remember when she'd felt it before. When both the feeling and the whirlwind passed, she staggered up against a table to catch her balance, her hair hanging in her eyes. She blinked around. She was in her own bedchamber now.

The room was sparkling clean. There was fresh water and food for Rufus. The rug had not only been swept, but the snags from Rufus's claws had been repaired. There were fat, silk-covered pillows lying atop the fat, silk-covered new featherbed, and a velvet coverlet was folded across it.

Rufus, sitting in the middle of the rug, looked alarmed. He, too, had been cleaned. His fur was fluffy, his feathers gleamed, and the tassel at the end of his tail had been combed and curled. He sneezed, and a few soap bubbles came out of his nostrils.

Celie walked over to Rufus and stroked his sleek head

to reassure him. When she straightened up she saw the door next to her wardrobe.

It was tall, and bound with iron, and Celie had never seen it before in her life.

She opened it with caution, and found a spiraling flight of stairs that led to a large tower room. The new room was empty except for tightly woven straw floor mats and assorted toys. It had broad, tightly shuttered windows on all sides, and a high, peaked roof. There was even a second water dish and box of sawdust.

"Oh, Rufus!" Celie called down the stairs to where the little griffin was doing his best to follow, but his freshly shined claws were slipping on the stone steps. "Come and see your new exercise room!"

Chapter 11

Lulath picked up JouJou and plopped her down atop the table in the schoolroom. "My own Lilah, say that you will see JouJou as the very queen of the Grath," he instructed. "Now say to greet her majesty!" He rattled off a complicated Grathian greeting that included praising both the queen's wardrobe and her many children, and ended with a comment on the weather that, to Celie's ears, made it sound as though the queen controlled the weather.

Lilah began dutifully repeating, and Rolf nudged Celie.

"What's going on with you and the griffins?" Rolf said in a loud whisper.

The hair on the back of Celie's neck stood on end, and her palms slicked with sweat. "What?" she choked out. Seeing Master Humphries looking at her, she managed to lower her voice. "What griffin? What are you talking about?"

"Aren't you looking for griffins in the library?"

"What? No!" Celie saw a vision of Rufus in the library, tearing apart priceless books and chewing on historic scrolls. "There are no griffins in the library . . . I mean, I'm not looking for griffins!"

Rolf raised one eyebrow at her babbling. "Bran said you were looking for stories about griffins," he clarified. "But I guess he was wrong . . . ?"

"No!" Again Celie had to lower her voice. Lilah was now discussing the weather with JouJou. "I *am* interested in stories about griffins. Have you found a book about them or something?"

"A book? No," Rolf said. "But I wondered if you wanted to see my cushions."

"Your . . . cushions?"

"And now the Celie will greet the queen," Lulath said with uncharacteristic sharpness.

Celie yanked her attention back to Lulath, and realized that he was looking at her with as much sternness as the normally silly prince could muster. Master Humphries, standing behind Lulath, was looking disapproving as well. Celie tried not to wince. She looked at JouJou—the queen—and tried to remember how to greet her.

"*Mineer othalia*," she began after taking a deep breath.

She relaxed when she saw Lulath smile and nod encouragingly. The queen scratched herself behind one ear and tried to hop off the table, but Lulath hauled her back into position as Celie continued, praising her furry majesty and then finishing with a question about whether it would be good weather for sailing next week.

Rolf's turn speaking to the queen took them to the end of their lesson, and then Rolf and Lilah left with Lulath and his dogs. Celie had to endure another afternoon of epic poetry, and this one with no mention of griffins to liven up the transcribing. She was also called upon to do some mathematics, and finished her lessons with a rousing recitation of her own lineage back to the royal barber who became Glower the Sixty-ninth.

After a quick check on Rufus, who was playing happily in his new tower room, Celie searched the Castle for Rolf. She found him just leaving the throne room with their father. She wasn't sure she even wanted to say the word "griffin" in front of King Glower, in case it made her blush or act in a suspicious manner, but her father was obviously preoccupied. He called her Lilah, slapped Rolf on the back so hard he nearly knocked his younger son down, and then wandered off, muttering something about speaking to the Council in their chambers.

"Is he all right?" Celie asked Rolf, staring after their father.

"Just worried about things going wrong with the Castle," Rolf said, his voice tinged with concern as well. "Do you want to see the cushions?"

"What cushions are you talking about?"

"The cushions in my bedroom have griffins on them,"

Rolf said, leading the way to his room. It wasn't far, now that all the bedrooms were in a row leading off the main hall. "I've had them for so many years, I hardly noticed them. In fact, I was going to ask Ma'am Housekeeper for some new ones, but when I heard that you were looking for griffin stories to read, I wondered if you wanted to see them first. They tell a story, sort of."

"Really?"

Celie followed him eagerly into his room. Rolf had a wide bench built into the bay window that filled one wall, and there were a number of cushions scattered across it. They were made from old tapestries, and Celie had sat on them many times without paying much attention to them.

"They're all from the same tapestry," Rolf said. "Ma'am Housekeeper told me that it was probably one that got too worn to hang anymore, so they cut out the parts that weren't totally threadbare and made them into cushions. Here, let me put them in order for you."

He scrambled the cushions around for a moment, then stepped back. There were six of them, all roughly the same size, and all faded and worn. Celie could understand why Rolf was looking for some new ones.

But if you looked beyond the shabbiness, you could see the griffins. Beginning on the left, Celie stood with her hands clasped and her mouth slightly open, seeing the life of a griffin depicted with rich threads.

The first cushion showed two halves of an egg with a

small griffin crouched inside, humans standing over it with arms outstretched as if greeting it. On the second cushion the griffin had doubled in size and played with a hound at the feet of a woman holding a lute and wearing an oddly draped gown. The third cushion showed a man in an enormous hat fitting the now full-grown griffin with a harness, and the fourth cushion showed him mounted on the griffin, gesturing with a stiff arm as though encouraging it to fly. The fifth cushion depicted a battle between knights mounted on griffins, and the sixth showed the griffin, fallen, while a man stood over it with hanging head.

"That one's sort of horrible," Rolf said apologetically, pointing to the last cushion. "There are a lot of arrows stuck in that poor beast. I usually turn that one against the wall."

"Yes, those are a lot of arrows," Celie said, not trusting her voice.

If the cushions were showing the life of a real griffin that had once lived in the Castle, she wasn't sure how she felt. The idea of Rufus flying excited and terrified her, much like the idea that he might be large enough for a grown man to ride on one day. She was charmed by the picture of the griffin playing with the dog, and hoped it boded well for Rufus to one day join the court without Lulath's dogs needing to fear that he would attack them. But the images of the battle and the slain griffin were deeply disturbing.

"We have to show these to Bran," Celie said, feeling almost overwhelmed.

She wondered what other evidence of the existence of griffins she had missed over the years. Suddenly she remembered that she still hadn't gone to take a good look at the tapestries that she had told Bran about, and wondered if Rolf knew about them. She tried to school her features as she turned to look at her brother, not wanting to make it seem too important, but Rolf was already watching her carefully.

"What are you up to, Cel?"

"Nothing," she said primly. "Well, something. It's a project for Bran," she added, in a less convincing tone. "He wants to know about any connection between griffins and the Castle. Can we take these to him?"

"Sure," Rolf said, shrugging one shoulder. "Maybe it will inspire the maids to bring me some less raggedy cushions."

They gathered up the cushions and made their way to the Armor Gallery, where Bran and Pogue were normally to be found. But the door was locked, and no one came to answer when Rolf knocked. Celie put down her cushions and peered through the keyhole, but the room was dark.

"They're not there," she said in disappointment.

"Well, back to the old window seat, I suppose," Rolf said cheerfully. "We'll have Bran come look at them after dinner."

But as they crossed the main hall, there was a commotion at the front doors. Looking around, Celie saw Bran and Pogue there, and beyond them a strange carriage coming to a halt in the courtyard.

"Who is that?" Celie asked Rolf.

"Let's see, shall we?"

Rolf glanced around, then tossed his armload of cushions through the broad arch into the dimness of the holiday feasting hall. With a pang of guilt, Celie did the same, and then followed her brother to the open doors. They stopped on either side of Bran, who Celie saw was clenching his fists nervously in the sleeves of his robes.

"What is it?" Celie asked in a low voice.

Bran shushed her.

A very tall, gaunt man in rich velvet robes stepped out of the carriage. He looked around the courtyard, his face pinched. Then he mounted the steps, studying Bran, Rolf, and Celie all the while. His eyes flickered over Pogue and then past him, as though he didn't exist.

"Good afternoon," Bran said. "I had expected Wizard Levin . . . I'm afraid I cannot remember your name, my lord wizard."

Celie didn't know wizards called each other "my lord wizard." And Bran was the Royal Wizard, besides! She didn't like how nervous this strange wizard was making her oldest brother.

"I am Wizard Arkwright," the gaunt man announced. "And I am here to help you fix this Castle."

Chapter 12

Celie's protestations that the Castle didn't need fixing had nearly gotten her banished from dinner, so she held her tongue. There was just something she couldn't like about the painfully thin, gray-haired wizard. He was watching them all with heavy-lidded eyes, as though measuring their worth—even the king's. Bran had asked for another wizard, his teacher Wizard Levin, to help catalog the weapons in the Armor Gallery, but Arkwright had taken it upon himself to come instead and study the entire Castle, not just the gallery.

It seemed very high-handed of Arkwright, and Celie decided to listen to him as carefully as she could. At dinner it appeared that Rolf and Lilah seemed much of the same mind, though Lulath was overjoyed to find that the new wizard spoke fluent Grathian, and had lived there for some years.

Lulath's dogs, on the other hand, clearly shared Celie's concerns.

"JouJou! Niro! Kitsi! You must be the behaving dogs!" Lulath said rather desperately as three of his girls attempted to attack Wizard Arkwright during the soup course. The fourth, Bisi, sat in Lulath's lap and growled across the table at the wizard, who ignored them all.

"Do you perhaps have a cat, Wizard Arkwright?" Queen Celina sounded on the verge of laughter.

"No," the wizard said in a dry voice. "I find that animals hinder me in my travels."

"Ah, most wise," King Glower said loudly, to drown out the yapping.

"I am so the embarrassments," Lulath said, his face crumpled with misery. "I have not the faintest why they must do so! They are the sweet little girls, always!"

"Animals don't like me," Arkwright said coolly. "I am not bothered by it."

Celie felt her eyebrows crawling toward her hairline, and tried to keep her face smooth. Then she looked across the table and saw her sister's stunned expression. They exchanged a look: What kind of person wasn't bothered by something like that?

"As soon as dinner is over, Wizard Bran, I'd like to see the Armor Gallery and begin my work," Wizard Arkwright went on.

Celie noticed that Wizard Arkwright was barely eating his dinner. He cut everything into small pieces and wiped his mouth thoroughly after each bite, which made it look like he was eating more than he was, but it didn't fool Celie. She was an expert at making it look like she'd eaten things she didn't like. Fish, for example.

Arkwright didn't fool Queen Celina, either. She was a queen, but she was also a mother, and knew what mealtime deception looked like.

"Wizard Arkwright," the queen said gently. "If the food is not to your liking, we could order something else from the kitchens for you. And please let Cook know if you have any special needs. We are so pleased that you have come, and we must do everything in our power to make you comfortable."

Lulath, who had finally gotten his dogs calmed down, eagerly pointed out that he himself did not eat meat, and that Cook had become very adept at preparing wonderful meals for him in the Grathian manner. He offered his own plate to Arkwright, urging him to sample the delicately prepared mushrooms he had been served, but Arkwright refused.

"I do eat meat," the older wizard said stiffly. "But I . . . have never had a large appetite . . . and as I get older I find it dwindles even further."

"Well, if there's anything you fancy, please let the kitchens know," Queen Celina said. "They will be happy to accommodate you."

"Thank you. Your Majesty is very kind," Arkwright said.

He looked uncomfortable, Celie thought. And she had

to grudgingly give him the benefit of the doubt. He was newly arrived in a strange place, and having everyone staring at him as he discussed his stomach must have been embarrassing. Celie let herself relax just a bit.

After dinner, she and Rolf went to the holiday feasting hall and arranged the tapestry cushions in order on the table. By silent agreement, they would not be taking them to Bran's chambers or the Armor Gallery. Celie had seen Rolf's face during dinner, and knew that he didn't like the looks of the new wizard, either.

"We'll just have to find a way to get Bran alone," Rolf said. "Or maybe we should take these back to my room. Or even yours."

"Not mine," Celie blurted out. "I mean . . . they're your cushions, you should keep using them until you get new ones anyway." She had visions of the cushions being gutted by Rufus.

"Seems like a shame to hide them away again," Rolf said. "Here they are easier to look at, and there's loads of candles in that box over there. Do you think you could ask the Castle to put a door in, instead of that archway? Keep everything safe?"

"I could try," Celie agreed.

Though the Castle hadn't done anything since, she was still feeling very pleased with Rufus's new tower playroom and the way the Castle had immediately responded to her pleas.

"It won't work," said a voice from the archway. "There has never been a door here." Wizard Arkwright gestured to the threshold as he stepped past it into the room. "The Castle could make it, but it would only be temporary. What are you trying to hide in here?"

Celie felt herself go hot, then cold, then hot again. Rolf was frankly gaping at the wizard. What did he know about the Castle? And how?

"We're not hiding anything," Rolf said after a minute. "We're just looking for a place to put these cushions where they won't be disturbed."

"They're for a project with our tutor," Celie added. She didn't want Arkwright to know that they wanted to show them to Bran.

"Surely the crown prince is too old to still be under a tutor's guidance?" Wizard Arkwright raised his eyebrows. Celie noticed, distracted, that his forehead was very high, and he could move his eyebrows a lot farther than anyone else she knew.

"Well, I thought I'd do some extra studying," Rolf said, making a flippant gesture. "I'm learning Grathian, a few things like that."

"Embroidery?" Impossibly, Wizard Arkwright's eyebrows went even higher. He looked down his long nose at the cushions.

"Epic poetry," Celie said, thinking of the poem she'd transcribed a few weeks ago.

"I see," Arkwright said. "Perhaps you should take these things to the schoolroom, then." He looked around at the crates of decorations. "This room has other purposes."

"How do you know we have a schoolroom? Or that this isn't it?" Celie stuck her chin up, not caring if she sounded rude.

"I assumed that you didn't sit on dusty crates to do your sums. Your Highness," Wizard Arkwright said just as rudely.

"The schoolroom's a bit crowded with some other things at present," Rolf said, poking Celie in the back. "We'll just leave them here for now and see what Master Humphries wants to do with them later." He stopped poking and took Celie's arm. "Come along, Cel, nearly time for bed."

"May I take these cushions?" Arkwright asked. "I merely wish to look at them." There was a sly tone in his voice.

"I'm sorry," Rolf said brightly, "but I'm sure Master Humphries will be along in minutes to see them. Good night!"

"Good night, Your Highnesses," Wizard Arkwright said, bowing his head just a fraction of an inch.

"Good night," Celie said from between gritted teeth.

"And if I may suggest, the poetry of Karksus is quite . . . evocative," he said as they walked by.

"Good to know," Rolf said, giving him a jaunty salute.

"I don't like him," Celie whispered as they walked across the main hall to her room.

"Nor do I," Rolf said cheerfully. "But the way I see it, he can't be worse than Khelsh and the old Emissary, and we got rid of them."

"No," Celie said. "Rufus and the Castle got rid of them."

Rolf just shrugged. "We still have the Castle," he pointed out. "And if we need to, I suppose you could summon a new Rufus!" He winked at her and said good night.

She went into her room, locking the door carefully behind her. Then she went up the wide spiral steps to Rufus's new tower. He was savagely tearing apart one of his leather balls, but when he saw her he dropped it and came running. He looked like he'd grown during dinner, but he was still ungainly and nearly tore the hem of her gown in his exuberance.

"We already have a new Rufus," she said aloud. "But I don't know how much help he'll be!"

Chapter 13

Celie could not stop thinking about what Wizard Arkwright had said about the holiday feasting hall. Of course it had other purposes; it had never occurred to her before, but now it seemed quite silly to think that there was an enormous room in the Castle that existed only for one week a year.

But it reminded her of what she and Rolf and Pogue had talked about when the hall first appeared, and what Bran had said at dinner that same night, about where the rooms of the Castle were before they were in Sleyne. Celie couldn't shake the feeling that the rooms were not only some*where* else, but with some*one* else.

Who had put the decorations in the boxes? Who had provided the food at the winter holidays? She'd always thought of it as just being "the Castle," but what did that mean? Somewhere, in a distant, exotic place, was there a kingdom where they had the other rooms of the Castle? Was there another throne room, another main hall . . . other towers . . . other kitchens?

She thought about the new kitchen, and the new stables. Had those other people used them until one day they were suddenly gone? Did they need the kitchen? The stables? Why had the Castle brought them to Sleyne, then?

Did these other people know about Sleyne?

She had been throwing a ball for Rufus up in his tower. She tossed it as hard as she could, so that it banged against the far wall, to give herself a moment to think. Was the Castle *stealing* from the other people for her family? Did it like them better, so it took away the others' holiday feast every year? Took away their best rooms, their furnishings, their stockpiles of silk and velvet?

Why was it doing this?

Sensing that she was distracted, Rufus took his ball back across the tower and began tearing it apart. Celie finally roused herself and hurried over to him. He had his wings hunched up and was trying to hide beneath them. He'd ripped up two balls so far that week, and sometimes it took the Castle a couple of days to provide a new one. Besides, it was hard to clean up all the lamb's wool stuffing and bits of leather.

"Give it to me," Celie said, snapping her fingers at him. Rufus ignored her. "Come on, give it!"

She looked around and spotted another toy the Castle had sent. It was made out of fur and looked like a squirrel that had been flattened. She ran over and picked it up, going toward Rufus with the flat squirrel in one hand. She clucked her tongue and shook the toy at him.

"Here, boy! Have Flat Squirrel! Flat Squirrel is funny! Let's play with him!"

Rufus took one look at the thing hanging from her hand and stopped tearing up the ball. He backed away from her, cowering, making a weird whining noise.

"What's the matter, Rufus?" She kept walking toward him, concerned now. "Come here, boy! What's wrong?"

It dawned on her that his yellow eyes were fixed on the toy in her hand, and that was what he was backing away from. She put it behind her back, and he visibly relaxed. She tossed it behind a wicker chest that she kept his food and toys in, and he immediately bounded around her, clacking his beak happily.

"So, you're terrified of mashed squirrels?" Celie was temporarily diverted from her disturbing questions about the Castle. "That's interesting."

Down the stairs in her bedchamber, she heard the door slam. She stiffened.

"Celie?"

"It's just Bran," she told Rufus, who had sensed her nervousness and let out a caw of alarm. "We're up here," she called down the stairs. She heard him make a muffled exclamation, and he started up the stairs. "This is the funniest thing; watch what happens if I show him that squir— You're not Bran!"

She ended in a shriek, leaping backward as Pogue entered the tower with a stack of books in his arms. He froze for a moment, and then dropped the books with an oath when he saw Rufus. Rufus, for his part, extended his wings and let out a scream of rage at the intruder.

"What is that thing?" Pogue shouted. He looked like he was torn between defending Celie and running for his life.

"How did you get into my room?" Celie demanded.

"What? I came in through the door!" Pogue was still shouting. "But what is that thing?"

Now Pogue did take a few steps farther into the room and put his big, calloused hand on Celie's shoulder, trying to tug her behind him and to the stairs. She didn't budge, though, and Rufus let out another angry cry when he saw Pogue touching his beloved Celie.

"It's okay, Pogue, it's just a griffin," Celie said, hoping to calm both Pogue and Rufus before someone heard Rufus's cries. "Rufus, be quiet!"

"*Rufus?*" Pogue was still trying to move her away from the griffin. "You mean it came back? After it ate Khelsh?"

"No, he's a new one. I hatched him from an egg. He's not dangerous!"

Rufus kept on sounding what Celie guessed was some sort of griffin war cry, and he was either going to permanently deafen her or rouse the entire Castle. His fur stood on end, and his wings were still raised. She ducked under his left wing and ran to the wicker chest, retrieved Flat Squirrel, and held it aloft.

"Rufus! Be quiet!" Celie put all the command she could into her voice.

He turned, saw Flat Squirrel, and immediately cowered back.

She blew her sweaty hair out of her eyes. Then she waved the toy again. "Now, sit!"

Rufus sat.

"What is that thing?" Pogue asked.

"I told you, it's a griffin," Celie said, impatient.

"No, that thing in your hand. It looks like a dead squirrel," he said with revulsion.

"Oh, it's a . . . toy squirrel," Celie told him. She put it behind her back before Rufus started whining. "Rufus is afraid of it, for some reason."

"Oh." Pogue sagged against the door that led to the stairs. "Now, please tell me: How long have you had a griffin, and why isn't everyone talking about it?"

"No one knows except Bran," Celie said. "And you have to swear that you won't tell anyone, either." She looked him in the eyes. "Promise me, Pogue. You have to help me protect him."

"But Bran knows?"

"Bran knows."

"All right, I promise," he said. "But . . . you hatched it? Did you . . . sit on the nest?"

Celie sighed. She picked up Rufus's ball and began to toss it for him again while she related the story of finding the egg. Pogue listened with his mouth slightly open, and when she was done, he sank down on his haunches. He held out a hand to Rufus, who crept forward and nibbled at his fingers playfully.

"A griffin," Pogue said in awe. "A real, living griffin."

Rufus bit him.

"Ouch! Nasty little—"

"Rufus! Don't make me get Flat Squirrel!"

Rufus decided to ignore Pogue and went to the far side of the tower to see if there was anything interesting in his food bowl. Celie bent down and picked up one of the books that Pogue had dropped.

"What is this?" It looked like a bestiary, a description of animals from all over Sleyne.

"Bran asked me to bring you these," Pogue said. "I didn't understand why, before. He told me to tell you to look for anything about 'our friend's family' in them." He pointed at the griffin, who was now drinking noisily, splashing water everywhere. "I still can't believe you have a griffin in your bedroom. Well . . . in your tower." He looked around. "Actually, I didn't know you had a tower of your own. I don't remember seeing this one before. Wouldn't it be right above the main hall?"

"I don't think you can see it from the outside," Celie said, though it dawned on her that she hadn't tried to look. "You shouldn't have been able to come into my room, either. Bran put a spell on the door to turn people away."

"Huh. Maybe it didn't work because Bran is the one who sent me."

"I suppose," Celie said. "Or maybe the Castle is okay with people finding out about Rufus now."

She looked around hopefully. The door at the top of the stairs swung shut, and she sighed.

"I guess not."

Pogue looked alarmed. "Did the Castle just slam that door?"

"Yes," Celie grumped. "It gets upset if I even hint about telling someone."

"I've never actually seen the Castle do something . . ." Pogue's voice trailed away. "Well, I suppose, with Khelsh and all that. But I have never seen it make something *move*." He was now looking at the door with the same fixation that he'd given Rufus.

"It's been very loud about what it wants and doesn't want me to do with Rufus," Celie said absently.

She had picked up the other books. In addition to the bestiary, there was a book of poetry and one of history. She remembered the poet that Wizard Arkwright had mentioned the night before, but couldn't think of the name. It had been a foreign name, certainly not one from Sleyne.

"Pogue, what do you think of Wizard Arkwright?" Celie asked.

"He's clearly very skilled, and very respected," Pogue said, but he was scowling despite his diplomatic tone.

"You don't like him, either?"

"No," Pogue said, shaking his head. "No, I don't. He's

not here to help Bran, he's here to check up on him, and I don't know if the Council of Wizards knows it."

"Why would he want to check up on Bran, then?" Celie was mystified. "Bran hasn't done anything wrong. He hasn't even been Royal Wizard long enough to do . . . anything."

She felt disloyal saying it, but it was true. Bran mostly read books, and occasionally made up healing potions for people in the Castle or the village who needed something stronger than the local physician could provide.

"Maybe Arkwright wants to be the Royal Wizard," Pogue said, shrugging. "Or maybe he wants to be the one to find out all the secrets of mysterious Castle Glower. It's too early to tell."

"What will we do?" Celie felt a cold lump in her stomach. She had enough to worry about already, and now this!

"Celie," Pogue said, tearing his attention away from Rufus and getting a good look at her face, "it's fine!" He gripped her arm with one large hand. "Don't worry. Bran can take care of himself, and besides, so far Arkwright hasn't done anything but be slightly rude at dinner. Maybe he's just making sure Bran succeeds as the new Royal Wizard. Bran's a little nervous about having him here, because Arkwright is one of the finest wizards alive. But he's not worried about Arkwright trying to do something nefarious."

"Nefarious?"

Pogue blushed. "It's a good word," he said, defensive.

"It *is* a good word," Celie said.

She felt awkward, and it was plain that Pogue did, too. He took his hand off her arm and cleared his throat. He took the heavy stack of books from her and started to carry them down the stairs. It was almost too much for Celie to take in. Rufus, Wizard Arkwright, the strange behavior of the Castle, and now here was Pogue Parry, the village flirt and troublemaker, using words that Bran would use. Words that Bran would use, and that Rolf would then mock Bran for using.

But Pogue had been spending a great deal of time with Bran lately . . .

"Pogue," she said, following him down the stairs. She snapped her fingers, and Rufus came at her heels. "What do you think about all these new rooms? Like the holiday feasting hall, just sitting there all the time. Where do you think they come from?"

Pogue put the books on her table. He stood with his back to her, flipping idly through the bestiary, and for a moment Celie wasn't sure that he'd heard her. Then he turned around, and his face was grave.

"I don't know," he said. "But I have a terrible feeling that if we don't find some answers soon, things could get very, very bad."

Chapter 14

After Pogue found out about the griffin, Celie continued to test the Castle's commitment to keeping Rufus a secret, especially around Rolf. After all, Rolf was the one interested in finding any stories about or pictures of griffins. Twice she said the name Rufus in front of Rolf, but both times, a door slammed loudly nearby, and he thought she was talking about her old toy anyway. This was both good and bad, as it protected the new, living Rufus, but it also made Celie seem to be childishly obsessed with her lost stuffed lion.

She was standing with Rolf in a long, little-used corridor with a couple of lamps, looking at the tapestries on the wall. They depicted a trio of hunting scenes, and the tapestry in the middle had griffins hunting deer while a group of women in faded gowns looked on. Celie had said, without thinking, that the largest of the griffins looked like Rufus.

"You know, Cel, you could get one of the seamstresses

to make you a new one," Rolf said at this third mention. "I bet they could use some of those fancy fabrics in the new room, and even put wings on him for you."

"What? Nooooo," she said. "I'm, um, fine." She had a sudden vision of the real Rufus taking one look at the new toy and tearing it to shreds in a jealous rage.

"No shame in wanting Rufus back," Rolf said. "After all, he did save all our skins, when it came right down to it."

"Yes, yes, he did," she said, and found herself smiling at the memory for the first time. All the same, she hurried to change the subject. "We should have Lilah look at these gowns and tell us what century they're from." She held her lamp higher, squinting at the faded images.

"True," Rolf agreed. "She'll probably know exactly what year that weird veil thing on her head was the fashion." He indicated one of the women, who had something that looked like a large, ermine-trimmed butterfly perched atop her yellow hair. "I think our sister is trying to make a name for herself as a clothing historian, though I'm not sure there is such a thing."

"Well, at least she's doing something," Celie said, then immediately felt a pang of sisterly guilt.

Celie was feeling unusually grumpy. At breakfast on Monday her father had asked her to turn the latest of her maps over to the court scribes, and she had reluctantly done so. Her father had told her not to worry about making any more. Because of the strange alterations to the Castle in recent months, the king had decided to summon the royal cartographer from whatever remote corner of the kingdom he had been working in to focus solely on the Castle until things "settled in."

Celie knew that her father had not meant to make her feel bad: the cartographer had already sought her out to commend her on her maps thus far. But all the same, she was feeling a bit confused. If she wasn't to be the official cartographer of the Castle, then what? As a princess—and a second princess, besides—she didn't have an important role in the court, and she'd been trying to make a name for herself with her atlas. Sensing her distress, Bran had quietly taken her aside after that breakfast and reminded her that this gave her more time to spend with Rufus. But no one was allowed to know about Rufus, which left her feeling fairly useless whenever she stepped out of her rooms.

"So, should we bring Bran and Lilah up here to see it, or should we try to take it to them?" Rolf asked.

Celie snapped out of her reverie and studied the tapestry. It was huge, and fastened up near the high ceiling, which would make it difficult to detach and carry around. But while bringing Bran up to look at the tapestry would work out fine, it meant that they wouldn't be able to lay the tapestry alongside the cushions to compare them.

"Let's take it down," she decided.

"How?" Rolf said. "I mean, I agree with you, but this is a pretty big tapestry."

"Well," Celie said, refusing to be daunted, "Bran *is* a wizard, after all. Let's see if he can find a way."

They made their way to the Armor Gallery, which was now quite a feat. Several of the main corridors no longer connected to each other, and one had to go around both the room full of fabrics and another large room that contained nothing but tables full of maps of strange places no one had ever heard of. Pogue had been right in predicting that room's location, and they were all hoping that the adjoining corridors he'd also spoken of would arrive soon. They would make moving through the Castle a great deal more convenient.

"Rolf," Celie said as they went down a short flight of stairs and then immediately up another set. "What do you think the Castle is doing with all these weird new rooms?"

"I don't know," Rolf said. "I'm sure it has its reasons, though."

"Yes, but what are they?"

They were on their way through the portrait gallery now, and Celie paused to scowl at one of their ancestors. Lilah had tried to tell her that she looked just like King Glower the Seventy-first, but Celie didn't see the resemblance, especially as Glower the Seventy-first had a large mole on his left cheek.

"Well, if it hasn't told you, it's certainly not going to tell me," Rolf said, shaking his head and laughing a little. "Let's just hope Bran figures it out before it becomes too difficult to navigate the corridors."

She had moved on to the next portrait, and was now studying Glower the Seventy-first's wife, Queen Elin. There was something about their faces that had caught Celie's eye, but she couldn't quite put her finger on what was so fascinating.

"You know, Cel, if you're interested in art, you should have Father find you a painting teacher. You've done an amazing job with your maps and sketches of the Castle with no training but what Master Humphries can provide. He's wonderful and all, but he's no artist. You're really good; you should get some better instruction."

"Thank you," Celie said, turning away from the portraits to smile at Rolf.

"I never can draw anything," Rolf said, shoving his hands in his pockets and continuing on through the long, narrow gallery. "My lines aren't straight, my circles are lopsided, and any time I draw a person's face it comes out looking like a duck."

"That's because you're trying to draw their eyes in the middle of their face," Celie said. She'd read several books on drawing. "Everyone thinks that you make an oval for a person's face, and then put the features evenly in the middle. But in reality, people's eyes and everything else are in the lower half of their— Oh!"

She stopped in the doorway of the gallery. Now she knew what had been bothering her about the portraits, and the tapestry as well. The people's faces. Or, more importantly, the fact that the people on the tapestry *weren't*.

"Weren't what?" Rolf gave her a baffled look as she said this last bit aloud.

"They weren't people at all," Celie said. "They were too tall and too skinny, and their faces weren't right. I don't think they're people like us."

"Hmm," Rolf said, leading the way down the corridor. They were almost to the Armor Gallery now. "You may have a point, Cel. The people on the cushions are a little weird as well. I'm curious to see what Bran thinks."

They would have to wait to talk to Bran, however. Pogue was there taking notes, which wouldn't have kept them from talking to Bran, but Arkwright was also with him, which did.

"Oh, er," Rolf said, "hullo there, Bran. Wizard Arkwright. Pogue. Just wanted to know if Bran had any spells for . . . tapestry removal."

"Tapestry removal?" Wizard Arkwright's eyebrows climbed his high forehead yet again. Celie reflected that he was almost as tall and strange-looking as the tapestry people. "Do you mean removing stains from a tapestry?"

"No, we, ah, need to move the tapestry itself, and it's rather large," Rolf said. He put his hands behind his back and grinned his most charming grin.

"Ah, the cushion project," Wizard Arkwright said.

"The cushion project?" Bran looked irritable. "What are you talking about?"

"Just wanted a bit of wizardry," Rolf said, still trying to look disingenuous.

Celie, however, was looking at Pogue. He was wiggling his eyebrows at her and seemed to be signaling for them to stop talking. Pogue jerked his head at Arkwright, whose back was to the young man, and then shook his head slightly. Then he cleared his throat.

"My sister, Jane Marie, would be glad to help," Pogue said when everyone looked at him.

"Oh, that's right!" Celie said, snapping her fingers.

Celie remembered that Jane Marie, who was roughly Lilah's age, was one of the finest embroiderers for miles around. She occasionally came to the Castle and helped to repair and restore the tapestries under Ma'am Housekeeper's watchful eye. Jane Marie knew a great deal about the symbolism that was often used in tapestries, like which flowers meant love or deceit, and other such things. Celie wondered what Jane Marie would make of the tall, strange people in the griffin tapestries. She grabbed Rolf's arm.

"Yes, we'll find Jane Marie," she said.

"We will?" Rolf looked surprised.

"We will," Celie said firmly. "And Ma'am Housekeeper. She knows how to remove the tapestries for cleaning."

They hurried out of the Armor Gallery, breathing similar sighs of relief when they were away from the beady gaze of Wizard Arkwright. Rolf sent a message for Jane Marie to come to the Castle at her earliest convenience, and Celie appealed Ma'am Housekeeper, begging the stern head of the household staff to have a crew of footmen remove the griffin hunting tapestry and spread it on the floor of the holiday feasting hall.

Jane Marie arrived while Celie and Rolf were overseeing

the rolling up of the dusty tapestry so that it could more easily be carried down the stairs and through the confusion of corridors to the holiday feasting hall. She appeared at Celie's elbow, giving a little cough over the dust clouding up from the tapestry, and startling Celie.

"Oh, goodness! Hello!" Celie turned red in embarrassment. Jane Marie was twice as particular as Lilah about her clothes and hair, if that were even possible. She smiled warmly enough at Celie, however.

"Hello, Princess Cecelia," she said in her soft voice. "Did you need me for something?"

"Why, yes!" Rolf came forward and bowed to Jane Marie. Celie felt her own eyebrows rising, and noticed that Rolf—Rolf!—appeared to be blushing slightly. "We've found the most beautiful tapestry, depicting a hunting scene with a griffin in it. It's the heraldic beast of Castle Glower, you know, and we wondered what insights you might offer us into the . . . er . . . sewing . . . and symbols . . . of the . . . item." He had begun rather grandly but petered out at the end, and Celie stifled a giggle.

"Oh, certainly," Jane Marie said, as if this were the most ordinary request in the world. "Where can I look at it?"

"We're moving it to the holiday feasting hall," Celie said, afraid that Rolf would get lost in his own words again. "We can lay it out across the floor there and have a look. We also have some embroidered cushions with griffins on them, if you wouldn't mind."

"That sounds very interesting," Jane Marie said, and

she showed her dimples to Rolf. "And if you're interested in griffins, you ought to come to the smithy sometime," she said, taking Rolf's proffered arm.

"Oh, really? Why is that?" Rolf asked, leading Jane Marie down the stairs. Celie came behind, feeling like a tagalong.

"Because there's the most beautiful image of a griffin carved into the side of the anvil," Jane Marie said. "And the anvil used to belong to the Castle, you know."

Chapter 15

The next day, Celie found the royal cartographer pacing outside her room. It was Saturday, and she didn't have lessons, so she'd been poring over the books Pogue had brought her. Rufus had been nipping at her for attention, and she'd decided to get them both a snack.

When she stepped into the passageway, the cartographer jumped a little, looking curiously at her door. Celie prayed that Rufus wouldn't scratch at it or let loose with his creaking war cry.

"I didn't notice that door," the man muttered. "Sorry, Your Highness." He bowed his head to Celie. "I have been looking for you, and I didn't know where—that is, I couldn't seem to find your room."

He looked embarrassed, and Celie reflected that it would be awkward to be the royal cartographer and have to admit that you couldn't find the first door on the right from the main hall. Of course, that was because of Bran's spell and not because the cartographer was in any way to blame, but she couldn't let him know that.

"How can I help you, sir?"

"Ah, yes." He looked even more embarrassed. "It's just that I wanted to have some sketches of the top of the Castle. The view from the highest tower, as it were."

"Yes?" Celie also thought this was a good idea—in fact, she thought it was a wonderful idea.

She had sketched the view of the rooftops from the Spyglass Tower during her long hours there the previous summer. But by now things were very different, and a map of the rooftops could prove useful. Particularly if one had to climb across them, as Celie had also had to do last summer.

"It's just that," the royal cartographer hedged, "normally, in my line of work, there are mountains, perhaps, but they're much larger and more . . . secure."

"Yes?" Celie was confused.

"Well, I know that you are more familiar with the roofs, and the towers, and I thought that you might . . ." At which point the royal cartographer's voice became so small and low that Celie couldn't understand him.

"What was that? Sir? I'm very sorry." Now she was getting embarrassed.

"I wondered if you might consent to, er, well . . ." Again with the near whisper.

"What?"

"Go up to the highest tower and sketch the roofs for me," he said in a rush.

"Me? Go sketch . . . You're afraid of heights?" Celie blurted out in incredulity.

"Yes, Your Highness," the cartographer said miserably. He couldn't meet her eyes. "I know it's shameful, a man of my age and in my line of work . . . But it's never been a problem before . . ."

"Not to worry!" Celie felt a leap of joy in her breast. To sketch her Castle again! To add to the atlas that she had begun! "I would be more than happy to do it! I know just the tower, too."

"Oh! Oh, thank you so much, Your Highness!" The royal cartographer was limp with relief. "I feel terrible asking you to do it, but it's such a relief to me, you cannot understand!"

He glanced up the corridor to make sure that no one had seen them, and Celie did, too. She knew, as she was sure he did, that her parents would put a stop to it at once if they found out. Also, it was extremely undignified for the royal cartographer to be asking a little girl to do his job. Even if she was the princess, and even if the job had once been hers.

"I do understand," she said. "And I'm happy to help. You go ahead and work on something else; I'll get you the sketches as soon as I can."

"Thank you again," he said, and bowed deeply.

He hurried away, and Celie waited until he was out of

sight before whisking back into her room, on the chance that Rufus was hovering just inside.

The griffin was actually across the room at her windows, perched on the long table where she studied and pecking at the latch on the shutters. He hunched his shoulders, hiding beneath the tent of his wings, and she sighed. He'd scraped up the latch, and had almost figured out how to lift it, she could see.

"Rufus! Get down from there!"

Celie intended to gather up her pencils and sketchpad as quickly as she could, before someone came along and asked what she was doing. She dumped her school things out on the table beside Rufus—who was taking up most of the table already—and stuffed any spare parchment, pencils, and soft erasers into her satchel.

Rufus hopped down from the table, snuffled at her bag, and then ran to the door. He looked back at Celie and made a little pleading noise, then turned around and began trying to lift the latch on the door. He was a lot better at this than he was at the window latch, and Celie watched with a plummeting heart as he flipped it up and opened the door.

"Rufus!" She lowered her voice. "Rufus, get back here!"

But Rufus crept into the corridor, wings hunched, head cocked to keep an eye on Celie as he went. She threw her satchel strap across her shoulder and headed after him. When she got into the corridor, he was already at Lilah's door. She grabbed his tail and tried to haul him back to her room, but the Castle closed the door, and she heard it lock.

"You're joking," she said aloud. "I'm supposed to take him with me?"

No answer except for her door staying locked.

Celie hesitated, shifting from foot to foot. She hauled Rufus away from Lilah's door, closer to the stairs at the end of the corridor, but didn't let him start up. Could the Castle really want Rufus loose? It would do him good: even with his tower to play in, he was bored and frustrated. And the Spyglass Tower would be deserted; he could perch in the windows and look out over the valley with her.

"All right," she said at last. "Come along! Hurry!"

She dropped his tail and started up the stairs, knowing that he'd follow. Sure enough, after a moment of surprise, he started up after her. She could hear his claws clicking and scrabbling on the stone steps, which were the tall and narrow kind.

But soon they were in another corridor, and another. Celie led him to the Spyglass Tower by the least populated route she could find. Twice she shoved him into a closet or an empty room, hiding with him and trying to keep him quiet while a footman or a councilor walked past. By the time they reached the steps to the tower, Celie was shaking with nerves. She chivied the griffin up the stairs and into the tower, and then leaned her back against the locked door, panting.

Rufus, on the other hand, was in his element. He squawked with delight over every new thing he found in the Spyglass Tower, from the last few hard biscuits in the tin to the large open windows.

"Hush," Celie said, but not with any real conviction.

She herself was sitting in one of the windows, her legs swinging free in the cold air and her sketchbook propped atop a musty cushion she'd found. She was busily sketching the landscape of Castle roofs, keeping only half an ear on Rufus's antics. He seemed fairly content to stand on a trunk and cry out, and she was soon taken up entirely in mapping out the top of the Castle.

It was soothing, really. Like one of the drawing exercises she'd studied in the book Master Humphries had given her a couple of years back, when she'd gotten serious about mapping the Castle. The roofs were all planes and angles; the towers were rectangles and cylinders with cones atop them. The roofscape, as Celie thought of it, was fun to draw—as long as one did not mind hanging out the window of the tallest tower, with cold wind whistling about one's ears.

And Celie did not mind. It was beautiful, with the clear, pale winter sky beyond the dark slate roof tiles.

"What are you doing?"

Celie nearly fell out of the window. A large hand grabbed the back of her gown and pulled her to safety at the last second. Rufus screeched, and the hand let go of Celie, who tumbled to the floor inside the tower. Looking up, dazed, she saw Pogue trying to fend off Rufus, who was attacking him with his front legs, beak, and wings.

"Pogue!" Celie wasn't sure whether to be relieved that it was someone who already knew about Rufus, or angry with him for scaring her like that.

"Get it off me!" Pogue yelled.

"Rufus, stop that!" She grabbed the edge of one wing and tugged. "Don't make me get Flat Squirrel," she threatened. "You know Pogue, now behave!"

Rufus couldn't resist giving Pogue one good bite on the arm, but then he subsided. Pogue rolled up his sleeve, but his tunic was thick enough to have prevented the griffin's beak from breaking the skin.

"Ouch," he complained. "I'm going to have a bruise!"

"Well, it's your own fault," Celie retorted. "What were you doing, sneaking up here and scaring us?"

"I wasn't sneaking," Pogue said, still rubbing his arm. "I was trying to find a place to be alone for a minute, so I came up here. When I saw you, I thought you were about to jump out the window, and I grabbed hold of you."

"Why would I jump out the window?"

"I don't know," Pogue said. "What were you doing, anyway?"

"I was sketching the roofs," Celie said.

"Why? I thought that was the royal cartographer's job."

"It is," Celie said, feeling guilty at revealing the cartographer's secret. "But he, ah, isn't quite feeling himself today."

Pogue obviously didn't believe her. He folded his arms and gave her a stern, big brother's look.

"He's afraid of heights and I'm not," Celie said. "Don't tell! I wanted to help with the atlas. It's *my* atlas, after all!"

That melted Pogue's stern demeanor. He uncrossed his arms and looked like he wanted to give her a hug or a biscuit or something.

"That's very true," he said. "It *is* your atlas. I'm sorry they took that away from you." He looked over her shoulder, staring out the window as he chewed the inside of his cheek.

Rufus, bored, started to inspect the corners of the room for more biscuits.

"What are you doing here, really?" Celie asked.

Celie had never heard of Pogue wanting to be alone. Ever. When he wasn't in the smithy, flirting with the village girls who came by to watch him work with his father, he was at the Castle with Bran or Rolf or Lilah.

Pogue looked around, and then seemed to realize how silly that was. They were quite plainly alone, in the highest, most remote tower in the Castle. He shoved his hands in his pockets and looked uncomfortable.

"I'm hiding from my father," he said in a low voice. "So that he won't make me work the forge today."

Celie wasn't sure she'd heard him correctly, so she waited a moment for him to say something else, or repeat himself, or give the punch line of the joke. But he never did. He just stood there in front of her, looking guilty and awkward and not at all like his usual self.

"Why don't you want to work the forge?"

"I hate it. I don't want to be a blacksmith."

Once again she thought she'd misheard. She hurried over to keep Rufus from trying to eat the eastern spyglass, and didn't see Pogue's face as he replied. And it was such a startling thing for him to say. But when she turned and saw his expression, she knew that she'd heard right, and that he'd meant it.

"But . . . but you . . . you've always . . ."

"My father is the best blacksmith for fifty leagues," Pogue said with a kind of grim pride. "And I am his only son. Of course I'm always at the forge. Of course I've been learning the trade since I could hold a hammer. But no one ever asked if I wanted to hold that hammer, and if I wanted to learn that trade." He smiled, but his face was still grim. "Just like no one ever asked you if you wanted to stop making maps and let someone else find the Castle's secret nooks and crannies."

Celie nodded. She understood completely.

"I feel like a coward," Pogue went on, "but I just can't face my father and tell him that I don't want to be him when I am older."

Pogue sounded young and uncertain, and so unlike himself. But Celie tried to act like Lilah or Rolf or Bran would, and listen to her friend. Even though she now wondered if he thought her a coward for not speaking up and telling her father that she wanted to keep on making maps of the Castle.

She stopped this uncomfortable line of thought with a question.

"So what do you want to do, if you don't want to be a blacksmith?"

Pogue fiddled with the biscuit tin for a moment. Rufus watched him intently, hoping for another biscuit, and when none was forthcoming, he tried to bite Pogue.

"Stop that," Pogue said, twisting out of the way of Rufus's beak. "Horrible beast!" When he found that Celie was still watching him expectantly, he sighed. "You have to promise not to tell anyone," he said.

"Promise," Celie said, crossing her heart.

"Well . . . I wanted to be a wizard, but I don't have the gift," Pogue said in a low voice. "So now I'm trying to become a wizard's assistant, at least. Or maybe a librarian."

Celie couldn't help herself: she laughed. It was just such a startling admission, coming from Pogue Parry. He had already graduated from apprentice to journeyman; everyone said he was even more talented than his father. Aside from blacksmithing, he seemed to like nothing better than to dance with pretty girls at all the festivals. The thought of him sitting in the library, wearing a patched robe and glaring at anyone who dared to smudge the page of a book, was ridiculous.

But the look on Pogue's face made her laugh die away quickly. He was hurt, and she felt the blood rush to her cheeks. Hot prickles of embarrassment ran down her sides and back. She reached out a hand to beg for him to forgive her, and ended up rubbing vigorously at the place where Rufus's feathers turned to fur, which always itched him.

"I'm sorry, I didn't mean to laugh," she mumbled. "It was just . . . I didn't expect you to say that."

"No one does," he said with a crooked smile. "At least, I'm assuming they won't expect it. That's why I haven't ever told anyone."

"Not even Bran?"

"Well, Bran knows," Pogue said. "He was there when I applied to the College of Wizardry." He shrugged. "But anyone can apply, and they promise to not even tell your parents, if you ask them not to."

Celie nodded. She knew this well. She'd applied to the College herself once.

Anyone over the age of five could meet with one of the testing wizards, who traveled all over the world, looking for children with magical gifts. It only took a few minutes; they asked your name and a few questions, but really, they were just seeing if their gift found a spark of magic in you.

Since Bran had the gift, Celie had wondered if she had it, too, and had met with the testing wizard who stayed at the Castle for a few days when she was six. He'd been very kind, had asked her about her birthday and whether she had a pet, and then smiled gently and told her that he was sorry, that she had gifts other than magic.

At first she'd been nearly bursting with excitement over the idea that she was special, that she had other gifts even more rare than magic. But over time she'd come to understand that that had just been his way of telling her that she wouldn't be joining her oldest brother in Sleyne City.

So she understood Pogue very well. She understood what it was like to have everyone think they knew you, and knew what you liked and what you wanted, but to secretly want other things, want to be different.

She almost started crying, but instead gave Pogue a tremulous smile.

"I'll keep your secret if you keep mine," she said, waving a hand at her sketchbook.

"It's a deal," Pogue said, offering his hand for her to shake.

She gave his warm hand two firm pumps, but when she tried to let go, his fingers locked around hers in panic. She looked up, and his eyes were wide, his mouth open. He was staring over her shoulder.

She wheeled around to see Rufus perched in one of the windows, stretching out his wings. He had to lean far out of the arch in order to get his wings free and extend them all the way.

"Now we're in trouble," Pogue said. "I think he's trying to fly."

Chapter 16

I'll help you get him back to your room," Pogue said, after he and Celie had wrestled Rufus down from the window-sill. "Will you be all right after that?"

"I guess so," Celie said.

She had both arms around Rufus's neck, and her heart was still thumping. The Spyglass Tower was at the northernmost point of the Castle, and from the north window, which Rufus had been about to leap out of, it was a sheer drop to a rocky gully. Rufus's golden body would have been a broken heap on the rocks far below, and it would have taken Celie nearly an hour to reach him. Of course, he might have been able to open his wings all the way and fly, but he was still so young and so clumsy that she doubted it.

"It'll be fine," Pogue said.

But he said it in a sort of frantic way, as if he were only trying to reassure her before he went off and had hysterics himself. He ran down the stairs ahead of her and Rufus, and checked to see if anyone was in the corridor. When he saw that it was clear, he signaled to her, and she and Rufus hurried after him.

"I'll just get you to your room," Pogue went on, leading them down the corridor at a fast clip. "And then I'm going to see Bran about something."

"Oh, okay," Celie said.

She felt like she and Pogue had just bonded, and now he was going to leave her? Now that Rufus had gotten the urge to try flying, she didn't know how she was going to keep him contained and amused, and she had been hoping that Pogue would stick around to play with him until he fell asleep.

"Don't worry," Pogue said as they ducked around a corner and hurried down another staircase. "I've got an idea that might help you. *And* Rufus."

And with that he left her at her door and went off to the main hall. Celie took Rufus into her room and locked the door. She went to her table to sort through what sketches she'd been able to make, when she realized that Rufus had gone upstairs to his tower. She couldn't remember if the shutters were latched or not, and raced after him to check.

They were latched, but Rufus was trying his best to get them open. He was ready to fly, and it seemed that nothing would deter him.

"Oh, sweetheart," she said. "Come here."

Something about her voice interested Rufus more than trying to get out of the tower, and he came over and leaned lovingly against her. He was the size of her old pony now, and she put her arms around his neck and sighed. If he grew as big as the griffins in the tapestries they'd found, he would be large enough for even a grown man to ride, and as difficult as a horse to hide.

"What am I going to do with you?" she murmured.

"You're going to train him properly," Bran said.

Celie wheeled around, clutching her chest. "Why does everyone keep sneaking up on me?"

"Sorry!" Bran said, almost as startled. "Sorry! I didn't mean to scare you!"

Rufus looked at Bran over Celie's shoulder and hissed.

"I didn't mean any harm," Bran said to Rufus. He held up his hands in a placating gesture.

"How are we going to train him?" Celie asked, surprising herself when she had to choke back tears. "What are we going to do? He needs to fly, but I'm so scared!"

"It will be all right," Bran said. He tried to hug Celie, but Rufus hissed again and he drew back. "Pogue found something that might help you, and he's working on it right now."

This diverted Celie from her tears. "What is it?"

"He's found a harness among the things in the Armor Gallery that we're certain is for a griffin," Bran said eagerly. "It looks exactly like the one the griffin is wearing on those cushions from Rolf's room that you showed me. But it's a bit big, since it's for a full-grown griffin, so Pogue took it to the forge to see if he could cinch up some of the straps and repair a broken buckle."

"A harness?"

"You can use it like a leash and collar, to guide him," Bran began, and then his face scrunched up. "Aaaaand . . . it looks like they also used it like a saddle . . . but at the very least we can guide him better."

"A saddle?"

"No, Celie," Bran said. "It's not a real saddle."

But Celie was thinking of the tapestries, and the griffins flying through the air with riders on their backs. The griffins were wearing some kind of harness, so that their people could hang on to them. The poem that she'd transcribed about the battle between the griffins and the Hathelockes had talked about fearless griffin riders, guiding their steeds through the sky.

"Do you think I could really train him?" Celie asked Bran. "And ride him?"

Bran looked alarmed.

"Listen, Celie," Bran began.

Someone knocked on the door.

Celie and Bran froze. Rufus started to investigate, but Celie dragged him across the room and shut him in the water closet, just in case it wasn't Pogue. When she opened the door she was glad that she had, because it wasn't Pogue; it was Rolf. Celie threw Bran an accusatory look—was the spell on her door wearing off? And then tried to summon a smile for her other brother.

"Yes?"

Rolf wasn't smiling, however. He looked grim. When

he saw Bran standing behind Celie, he gave a small nod and stepped into the room.

"Oh, good. You're both here," Rolf said. "Celie, I found that book you were talking about, the one with the epic poem that mentions griffins. Bran, you've got to do something about Wizard Arkwright."

"Why, what did he do now?" Celie demanded. "And where's the book?"

"That's just it," Rolf said. He walked over to a chair and sat down heavily. "He took it from me."

"He . . . took a book from you?" Bran said, puzzled.

"Yes," Rolf replied shortly. "Did you know that he hates it that Celie and I are collecting things with griffins on them, and putting them in the holiday feasting hall? He's in there all the time, rummaging around, moving the cushions, tripping over the tapestry and telling me that we really should put it back on the wall in the corridor before someone gets hurt or it gets ruined."

"It's true," Celie said, seeing the skeptical look on Bran's face. "I don't know what it is, but he interrupts us all the time. He wants the things we've gathered put back where they came from, and immediately."

"Well," Bran said, looking doubtful. "I mean, you can see why your project would be interesting to anyone. You took the anvil from the village forge, Rolf!"

"I only borrowed it," Rolf protested. "And they have another one. Besides, that anvil used to be here, in the Castle. So it really does belong here."

"Why did he take the book away from you?" Bran said.

He was trying to sound patient and grown up, but Celie could tell that even Bran couldn't entirely excuse the other wizard's taking of a poetry book.

Rolf ran his fingers through his hair. "I was in the library, trying to find anything about griffins we'd missed. I mean, it's so strange: Lilah has twenty-three books about unicorns just in her room—twenty-three! But there's nothing about griffins in a castle that has griffins on its banners? How do we even know what a griffin is if there's no books or pictures, just a few tapestries that no one but the family or the maids would have seen? Anyway, I had asked Master Charles if he knew of any books, but you know how he is. He always thinks you're just there to scribble rude words in the margins of ancient scrolls or something.

"Anyway, Pogue popped his head in to tell the old man that he was going to take some book home—and by the way, how come Pogue gets to borrow whatever he likes, but I get the evil eye? I'm going to be Glower the Eightieth, for heaven's sake!"

"Get on with the story," Celie cried out in frustration. She was starting to hear Rufus scratching and scrabbling at the door to his tower.

"All right!" Rolf threw up his hands. "When Pogue asked what I was looking for and I said, anything about griffins, he led me right to that epic poetry tome you described, Cel, and Charles actually let me borrow it. He also suggested some poet I'd never heard of . . . Caras? Anyway, I tried to bring the book I had to the holiday feasting hall, but Arkwright was standing right outside the library door. Scared me half to death! He said he was in great need of some bedtime reading, took the book right out of my hands, and disappeared to his rooms with it! Pogue is my witness," Rolf finished, holding up a hand as though swearing an oath. Then he frowned. "Er, he's my witness when he comes back from whatever errand he was running. He was in rather a hurry, muttering something to himself about buckles."

Bran and Celie exchanged looks.

"That's hardly sinister behavior," Bran said. "I mean, Arkwright's behavior. I'm sure I . . . don't know what Pogue is doing."

"Noooo," Rolf said. "Not really that sinister. But when you take into account all the times he's popped up, out of nowhere, to comment on our little project or to try to interfere, it starts to look like Master Wizard Arkwright does not want griffins talked about in the halls of Castle Glower!"

Rufus squawked. Loudly.

Celie sighed. Clearly they would have to tell Rolf. Bran gave her an encouraging nod, and Rufus started to scratch at the door as Rolf got to his feet.

"I feel better getting that off my chest," Rolf said, stretching. "I think I might have a bit of a snack before dinner." He cocked an eyebrow at Bran. "If you'll promise to get that book back for me? And keep an eye on Arkwright?"

Bran opened and closed his mouth a couple of times before saying yes.

"I'm not asking you to spy on a fellow wizard," Rolf said, moving toward the door to the corridor. He walked right past the door to Rufus's tower without looking at it. "But I swear, there's something off about him."

"I agree," Celie said faintly.

Had Rolf gone mad? Did he not hear the racket that Rufus was making now? Did he not notice the large iron-bound door that had not been in Celie's room the last time he'd been there?

"It's true that he wasn't supposed to be here at all," Bran said. His voice sounded normal, but he was staring at the door that Rolf didn't seem to be able to see. "And a lot of wizards are nosy, but he mostly ignores Father and does seem awfully curious about what you and Celie are studying with Master Humphries."

"Exactly!" Rolf said, pointing a finger at Bran. Then he tweaked Celie's hair ribbon and walked out of the room, whistling. "See you at dinner," he called over his shoulder as he went down the corridor toward his own room.

"That was . . . he didn't . . . He walked right by the door," Celie finally managed.

"I've never seen anything like that," Bran said. "It wasn't me; it must have been the Castle, which tells us something."

Celie was too stunned to puzzle it out by herself. "What?"

"The Castle really did want Pogue to see Rufus," Bran said. "But it definitely did not want Rolf to."

Chapter 17

He can't see," Celie fretted. "It's too dark! He's going to run right into a wall!"

"We really don't have much choice," Bran said. "And look how eager he is; he'll be fine."

It was true: Rufus was about to leap out into the cold night air, never mind how dark it was. They were in the tower where he had hatched, since it had nice wide windows and was on a side of the Castle where there weren't any bedrooms. They didn't want some late-working councilor to look out his window and see Rufus learning to fly.

"There's Pogue with the lantern," Bran said, pointing.

Far below them, a small light bobbed up and down, signaling. Pogue was standing in the empty back corner of the stable yard, which the new stable had blocked off. The only way to get to it now was to go through the new stable, which had taken Pogue longer than it had taken Celie and Bran to drag Rufus up to his hatching tower.

"I hope the harness isn't too heavy," Celie said.

She ran her hands over the leather straps and steel buckles one more time. The harness went around Rufus's chest and across his back, fastening under his belly and leaving his wings and legs free. There were two loops of leather at his shoulders that looked like handles for a rider to hold, but there was nothing resembling a saddle attached to it. Still, Celie thought that she would be able to hold on and sit comfortably behind his wings. If Bran would let her.

And if Rufus did learn to fly.

She knew she was fussing unnecessarily, but she just couldn't stop. If Rufus didn't learn to fly on the first try, he'd be dashed to bits on the stones of the courtyard at Pogue's feet. Birds did it all the time, but many of them died trying. Her stomach clenched, and she wished she hadn't eaten so much winter apple pie for dessert.

Her baby. Her little griffin. If he fell . . .

"Celie," Bran said. "Look at Rufus: he's ready."

"*I'm* not ready," she muttered. "Hey, now!"

She yanked on the harness as Rufus tried to tip himself out the window.

"Celie," Bran said, laying a hand on her shoulder. "If he falls, I will catch him. With magic. I promise."

She looked at her eldest brother, searching his face for signs that he was lying to make her feel better. "Promise?"

"Yes," he said. "I can make a sort of pillow of air under him," Bran assured her. "Also, I wonder if the Castle won't help. It's obviously eager to keep Rufus alive, and it caught you once, after all."

"That's true," Celie said.

With both Bran and the Castle (she hoped) ready to break Rufus's fall, Celie felt a lot calmer. She let go of the harness and took a step back.

"Go ahead, Rufus," Celie said, around the lump in her throat.

Bran flipped the shutter on their lantern so that the light wavered. It was their signal to Pogue, who raised his lamp high in answer.

Rufus didn't need any further urging. He leaped into the air, his wings extended, and soared into the night. Celie's heart was pounding, her knees weak, and she half fell against the window as she leaned out as far as she could to watch.

Rufus glided for a moment, and then began to sink and flap his wings. But his wing movements weren't coordinated, and he started to sink even more rapidly, listing to the right as he went. Celie's mouth flew open to scream, but she managed to get it closed and just whisper to her brother.

"Bran, Bran," she said, her throat dry. "Catch him."

"I will if he . . . before he hits," Bran said. He was crammed into the window beside her, face white with tension.

Then Rufus got the hang of it. His wings started working together, and he rose up a little. Then a little more. Then his wings cupped and he beat the air with powerful strokes, rising higher and higher. Celie let out a yell of delight, and Rufus screamed in triumph.

"Okay, Rufus," Celie said, trying to coax him back in. "That's enough for now."

"He looks like he's getting tired," Bran said. "Probably using muscles he didn't even know he had." He clapped his hands. "Come here, Rufus! Good boy!"

Rufus cawed and turned again, his wings still beating hard. He started away over the courtyard, occasionally dipping down but then frantically bringing himself up again. But with every passing moment he seemed to get more confident, more graceful, though Celie agreed that he was starting to look tired.

She called to him again, but he ignored her. He looked like he was going to try to fly out of the Castle entirely, going over the stables and the wall. But he wasn't going to make it. Despite his more confident flying, he was weakening and starting to sink lower. If he kept descending at that rate, he would run right into one of the crenellations at the top of the eastern wall.

Far below him, Pogue waved his lantern and whistled piercingly. Rufus looked down, and then slowly circled to land with a bump beside Pogue.

Celie collapsed on the floor of the tower, feeling a bit of the scattered eggshell crunch under her weight. She put her head on her knees and tried to get her heart under control.

"He did it," she chanted. "He did it. He did it."

"He did," Bran said, sounding just as relieved as she did. "He really did."

Her brother reached down and took Celie's arm, helping her to her feet. "Let's go down and congratulate him."

"All right," Celie said, still feeling shaky.

In the corridor outside the hatching tower, Bran stopped short. Holding his lantern high, he squinted at the tapestries on the wall. They were a different style from the others they'd found. Celie had passed them many times, but she was always in such a rush that she had never stopped to consider them. They were filled with griffins: Griffins hatching from flame-colored eggs. Griffins playing together in a forest, chasing after a ball. A small griffin taking flight from a tower while a dozen people below watched and applauded.

"I think that was his first flight," Celie said, stunned that she hadn't noticed it before. "These all seem to be . . . griffin nursery scenes, don't they?"

Bran snorted at her description, but then he grew thoughtful. "You know, I think you're right. These griffins are all smaller than the ones on the other tapestry. And they're all doing babyish things."

Celie slugged him in the arm. "That's what I said, they're nursery scenes," she said. "I wonder if we can drag these down to the holiday feasting hall."

"I don't think we should," Bran said. He jerked his chin, and they continued on their way to meet Pogue and Rufus.

"Why not?"

"Well, you already think that Arkwright is watching you. These tapestries . . . they're not like any others I've seen. They're very realistic, almost domestic. It will be hard to keep up the fiction that griffins are, um, fiction when people start seeing these."

"That's true," Celie said. "I mean, writing a poem about riding a griffin could be a poet's fancy. Making a tapestry about hunting with griffins instead of falcons, fancy again. Or even depicting parts of that poem."

"But baby griffins going about their day?" Bran finished the thought. "That makes you wonder whether the weaver had actual experience with griffins."

They continued in silence for a while, making their way down through the Castle without running into any-one. It was nearly midnight, and just thinking that made Celie yawn. Now that the strain of Rufus's first flight was over, she was noticing how tired she was, and how limp she still felt, and let herself lag behind just a little bit. She fol-lowed Bran out into the courtyard and past the stables.

As they ducked into the new stables, Bran held the lantern high and they looked around. It was shaped differ-ently than the old stables. The stalls were narrower, the partitions lower. It had a cold, unused feel, and the wood of the stalls was scarred and scraped, but the stable wasn't dirty. In fact, there was no straw or any other debris about.

Either the grooms had cleaned it thoroughly after it had appeared, or it hadn't been used for a long time before that.

Pogue met them at the back door of the stable, grinning broadly. He was holding his lantern with one hand and Rufus's harness with the other. When Rufus saw Celie, he lunged forward, and Pogue hurried to pull his hand out of the leather straps.

"Ouch!"

"There you are! My clever boy!" Celie ruffled Rufus's neck feathers and cooed to him, overcome with love and pride in her griffin. "You flew, you actually flew, Rufus!"

"That was a little hair-raising to watch," Pogue said, shaking his head in wonder. "I just kept hoping that if he didn't get his wings working, the Castle would catch him."

"So did we," Bran said. "I might have been able to do something, but . . ."

Celie looked up. "You *might* have been able to do something? You told me you could catch him! You promised that you could!"

Bran looked decidedly guilty. "It's very likely that I could have," he said. "But I didn't need to, and that's all that matters!"

Celie sagged against Rufus, continuing to pet him. "Uncle Bran lied," she told the griffin in a stage whisper. "But it's all right, because you're such a good boy!"

"Yes, yes," Bran said, rolling his eyes. "I lied. Now let's get Rufus back inside the Castle, shall we?"

Rufus reached over Celie's shoulder and began to gnaw

on the top of the nearest stall door. Celie took hold of one of the handles at his shoulders and gave it a little tug, clucking her tongue. She was trying a combination of horse and dog training with the harness, to get Rufus to obey better.

"Come along, Rufus," she said, and gave another tug.

He sighed and stopped chewing the door, following Celie. She glanced back to see if Pogue was following, and stopped. She turned and looked more carefully at the wood where Rufus's beak had left a strong impression. There was another mark next to it, just like the one Rufus had made, but obviously older and worn smooth.

The stall had a built-in water trough, but no manger for hay. Instead there was another bucket built into the corner of the stall, the exact size of the bowl the Castle had provided for Rufus's food.

"Are you coming?" Bran raised his lantern and peered down the aisle at her. Pogue was staring around at the new stable, too, a line between his brows. Celie caught his eye.

"This is a rather odd stable," he said.

"That's because it isn't for horses," Celie said, leading Rufus up the aisle toward them. "It's for griffins."

Chapter 18

They did a quick search of the griffin stable, but didn't find anything more interesting than the fact that it existed at all. Everything was clean and bare, and there was not a single indication that it was meant for any unusual purpose. Celie would never have noticed if Rufus hadn't bitten the wood of the door right next to the place where some other griffin, years ago, had bitten it.

"Bran," Celie said, her voice a little choked. "Do you understand? The tapestries of the griffin nursery—"

"What griffin nursery?" Pogue sounded almost panicky, but Celie ignored him.

"And now this," she went on. "Don't you see: Rufus isn't some spell by a wizard that went awry. He isn't some freak of nature. There really used to be griffins in Castle Glower. Ordinary, everyday griffins. But now Rufus is the last one."

Bran just nodded. He looked like he couldn't speak. Celie was, herself, on the verge of tears. She was so lonely for Rufus, being the last griffin. Pogue looked a little wild-eyed, and didn't say anything either as they walked back to the main courtyard, where he nodded good night and went home to the village.

In silence Bran and Celie sneaked Rufus back into the Castle. Celie fell asleep with Rufus cuddled up against her, after telling him once more how clever he was, and taking off the harness and hiding it under her bed. She hoped to let him fly even longer the next night, and the one after that, and dreamed of sailing through the night sky on his back.

But she woke to a storm in the morning, a late-winter blizzard that brought icy winds and heavy piles of snow that clogged the corners of the windows and made the stones of the courtyard treacherous.

Rufus hated getting wet, and he certainly couldn't make his second flight with the wind buffeting him back and forth, she thought with despair. Sitting in her lessons that day, she glumly wondered when the skies would clear, and whether Rufus would even remember how to make his wings work by then.

"You are all the best of Grathian speakers," Lulath enthused, spreading his arms wide.

Celie snapped her attention back to Lulath, who had just finished helping them through the last page of the

Grathian primer they'd been studying. He looked like he was near tears, and his dogs, sensing his emotion, were prancing in circles around his feet.

"I never thought, that here in the Castle of Glower, I would have so many, many of friends who would come to a learning of my language!"

Lulath swooped down and kissed them all, moving down the table to smack his lips against each of their cheeks, starting with Rolf. Rolf yelled in surprise, but didn't pull back, manfully patting Lulath's shoulder instead as Lulath kissed Lilah, then Celie. Then, to Master Humphries's horror, the prince grabbed him by the arms and kissed his cheek as well.

"Thank, oh so many times, for giving to me this chance!"

"You're very welcome," Master Humphries gasped out, straightening his robes.

"And now, the presents for my most best students," Lulath said.

With great ceremony he opened a canvas bag that had been sitting unnoticed in the corner of the room. From it he pulled a long blue silk scarf, which he presented to Lilah.

"The finest of the silk of Grath, in the color of the beautiful eyes!"

Lilah turned bright pink and took the scarf with reverent hands. "Oh, Lulath! It's so lovely!"

"I could not be waiting another moment's time to be

giving it," Lulath said, and actually blushed. "For Rolf, this best of Grathian steel," he announced when he'd recovered a bit. And he presented Rolf with a fine dagger in a tooled leather sheath.

"Thank you, Lulath," Rolf said in Grathian, and Lulath gave a little bow.

"For this master," Lulath went on, turning to their tutor, "so kind to let me take his lessons away, this ink and roc quill pens!" Lulath gave the flustered Master Humphries a set of quills and ink.

Celie craned her neck to look at the roc quills. They were black and strangely dense looking, as though they absorbed light. She'd never heard of roc feathers being used for pens before, but Master Humphries took them with the same delicate awe with which Lilah was holding her scarf. Celie remembered that rocs were becoming rare in Grath, and realized that the quills must have cost a small fortune.

Celie felt a flutter in her middle and wondered what gift Lulath had found for her. A scarf, too? Her eyes were more gray than blue, though, and sometimes looked rather washed out if she wore the wrong color. She supposed that he would give her something more suitable for a young girl, and gave a little sigh. She hated being treated like a child.

"And for the Celie," Lulath said, "a two things: a griffin of Glower, made by my own cousin, who is with the wood an artist."

And he set an intricately carved griffin the size of Celie's two fists in front of her. It was carved of blondwood, highly polished to bring out the golden sheen, and there were small topazes set in the eyes. The griffin was standing on three legs, with its right front claw extended and its wings raised.

"He looks just like R—" Celie stopped herself just in time. "Oh, thank you, Lulath," she said sincerely in Grathian.

"But also for the Celie, and the Rolf, too, is this," Lulath was saying. He took one last item out of the bag. It was a large and very old book. The leather cover was worn and the spine was cracked, and Celie could see that the edges of the pages looked slightly chewed.

"It is not the most beautiful of books," Lulath said. "But it is a book of the griffin and the Castle!"

"What?" Celie almost dropped the book as he handed it to her.

"Where did you get this?" Rolf wanted to know. He leaned eagerly across Lilah, who snatched her scarf out of harm's way as their brother put both palms flat on the table to boost himself up.

"It is the very oldest of old books," Lulath said. "It has for the many years lived in the library in the Grand Palace of Grath. But I think it belongs to here, to the Castle of Glower, and here must stay now."

"Lulath, thank you," Celie said in Grathian.

Her hands were shaking. She had turned to the title page of the book. The writing was faded, but she could make it out with a little effort. The book was a history, not of the country of Sleyne with small mentions of the Castle, but an actual history of Castle Glower itself. It had been written by one of the Royal Wizards over three hundred years ago.

"It is my pleasure, truly," Lulath replied smoothly in Grathian. "It belongs here, you know. I believe it was brought to Grath by a princess of Sleyne who married our king two hundred years ago, and I suspect that she was not supposed to take it with her. My brother found it, when I wrote to him and asked if he knew of any books about griffins." Lulath grinned his daft grin at Celie. "I have seen you two searching the Castle for legends of the griffins, and I know you are not having much luck finding any!"

Celie got up from her chair and went around the table to kiss Lulath.

"Thank you, Lulath."

"It is good to have friends," Lulath said, almost bashfully.

"And it's good that I understood all of that," Lilah said, delighted. "I can actually speak Grathian," she marveled, in Grathian.

Lulath continued to compliment them all about how well they could speak Grathian, but Celie wasn't listening. She had returned to her seat and was turning the pages of the book eagerly. She couldn't believe she had a book in her hands that talked about griffins. Not just a single mention in the line of a poem, but an entire book about griffins and Castle Glower.

"Whatever you do," Rolf said in her ear, "don't leave *that* in the holiday feasting hall. If Arkwright finds it . . ."

He didn't even need to finish that sentence.

"I won't," Celie said. "I am going to keep it in my room under lock and key. You and Bran and I are going to read this and find out what we need to know about the Castle and griffins and everything!"

"Well, I can see that I will not be able to have further lessons today," Master Humphries said, but he didn't look upset at all. "I really am very pleased with how well you are all learning Grathian, and could not be more grateful to Prince Lulath for teaching you so expertly!" He clapped his hands, applauding Lulath, who gave the tutor a little bow. "So perhaps we can end early today to celebrate. And I certainly cannot argue with Princess Cecelia's interest in a history book, which has taken all her attention!" Master Humphries smiled at Celie, who gave him a grateful smile in return.

She wrapped up her carved griffin and put it in her satchel with her school things and then left, the big history book hugged to her chest. Rolf followed her out of the schoolroom; Lilah, Lulath, and Master Humphries were talking about the Grathian seaside, which was apparently both beautiful and contained a small village that spoke entirely its own language.

"No one is asking them where they are coming from, or why it is the Grath they live in now," Lulath was saying as Rolf and Celie left. "Because no one is having the idea in slightness of what they say!"

"I have to admit," Rolf said as they went down the stairs, "I didn't think Lilah would stick it out. But she's just as good as either of us."

"I don't think we take her seriously enough sometimes," Celie said. "It's the flirting."

"And the hours spent on her hair," Rolf agreed. "Hard to remember that she has a fine brain, when all you can see is all that hair curled and shined and scented."

"Imagine if you *could* see her brain," Celie said, wrinkling her nose. "It would be extremely disgusting."

"True," Rolf agreed. "But if everyone's brain was on the outside— Oh, hello, Mother!"

Queen Celina was coming up the spiral staircase, looking anxious.

"Rolf! Celie!"

She hurried to meet them, but had to stand a few steps down and look up into their faces. The staircase was not wide, and it often made people feel claustrophobic, if too many tried to crowd up it at once.

"Do you know about the open tower at the top of the staircase?"

Celie's heart gave two irregular thumps, and she pressed the Castle history even tighter to her chest.

"At the top of which staircase?" Rolf asked.

"This one," their mother said, pointing straight up. "Past the schoolroom."

"There's nothing past the schoolroom," Rolf said. "The staircase ends there." He leaned his head back, trying to see up the stone corkscrew, and failing. "I mean, it just—hang on, does it?"

"It does," Celie said, but her voice sounded strange to her own ears, and her mother looked at her askance.

Celie's heart was beating even harder now. Had someone found Rufus's hatching tower? Her mother? One of the maids? And what did that mean? Did it mean that it was time for her to show Rufus to the rest of her family?

"I was on my way to the schoolroom," Queen Celina said. "I knew that you were finishing your Grathian lessons today and wanted to see how you were doing. But the stairs just kept going up and up. At the top is a corridor with a tower at the end, and in the tower is a giant nest full of eggshells!"

"Eggshells?" Rolf raised an eyebrow.

"But they're much too thick to be a bird's, and bright orange besides," their mother continued. "So I went down and got Bran and Wizard Arkwright." She turned and looked over her shoulder. "Here they are now!" She started up the stairs, forcing Rolf and Celie to turn and start back up. "Wizard Arkwright thinks they might be roc shells," Queen Celina said as they climbed. "But I have a different theory."

"Oh, yes?" Rolf was bounding up the stairs ahead of Celie, who did her best not to drag her feet and get stepped on by their mother or the wizards coming behind her.

"Oh, yes," Queen Celina said. "I think they're from a griffin."

Chapter 19

The hatching tower was freezing cold. Snow coated everything, and the moss and twigs of the nest were brittle and crackled under their feet as Queen Celina ushered them all into the round tower. Celie hoped that her shakiness would be taken for a reaction to the weather and not nerves. Bran kept wiggling his eyebrows at her, but she had no idea what he was trying to say.

A quick look around showed that the broom she had used to sweep away the snow and the blankets she had covered the egg with were scattered around, covered with ice and looking like they'd been there a hundred years, much to her relief. She didn't think they had any marks on them that would indicate they were new, or that Celie had used them.

"What's that book?" Pogue came huffing into the tower behind the wizards and stood next to Celie.

"It's nothing," she said, and now she wiggled her

eyebrows, willing him not to draw attention to the book with Arkwright standing so near.

But Arkwright wasn't listening to them. He was on his knees in the snowy ruins of the nest, prodding the bits of shell with one long finger. Queen Celina had swept her long skirts aside and joined him on the floor, cupping a jagged piece of the orange shell in her own hands.

"It's a griffin egg," Celie's mother said with a sigh. Her lips curved into a broad smile. "I can't believe it."

"Impossible," Arkwright said. "There's no such thing as a griffin."

His expression was stiff, and not just because of the cold. Celie thought that he looked like he wanted to say something else. She braced herself, ready to fling back an insult if he dared to say something cruel to her mother. Beside her she felt Rolf straighten as though he, too, were prepared to defend Queen Celina.

"It's far more likely that it's a roc egg," was all Arkwright said. He took out a handkerchief and carefully laid a few pieces in it. "Still worth investigating, of course. But I see no reason to cause such a fuss."

"Roc eggs aren't orange," Queen Celina pointed out. "Bran, what do you think?"

"What makes you think it could possibly be a griffin?" Arkwright said before Bran could answer, his expression pinched. "Might as well assume a dragon, or a salamander."

"Sleyne isn't exactly known for its salamanders," Queen Celina said with some asperity. "And my father once told me that griffins, which are generally golden in color, lay eggs that look like balls of flame." She held up some of the eggshell, which did have a flame-orange hue in the winter sunlight. "Bran?"

"Roc eggs are white, with brown and green speckles," Bran supplied. "Salamander eggs would be much smaller, and dragons are mythical."

Celie noticed that he carefully did not say it was or wasn't a griffin's egg.

"Whatever these are," Arkwright said, "they are undoubtedly very old. Who knows how many centuries they lay here before the Castle brought this tower to Sleyne?"

"I have a funny feeling they're not that old," Queen Celina argued. "Look at this nest: it's all frosted over, but if this moss were centuries old, it would be dust by now! And feel how sharp the edges of the shell are. If they'd been exposed to the elements for very long, wouldn't they have been worn smooth?"

She looked eagerly from Arkwright to Bran. The former just looked grave, but the latter was surprised into a nod. She pulled out her own handkerchief and began gathering up pieces.

"And look at this! There are still bits of yolk or whatever you want to call it on some of these. It would have been washed clean by now, you both know it!" Queen Celina sounded as though she were becoming more than a little put out with the two wizards, who clearly did not view her find with as much excitement as she did. "Celie, don't you think it's wonderful? Do you think it's a griffin egg?"

Celie let out a small squeak. They were all looking at her now, and once again Bran's eyebrows were moving.

"I—um—" Celie stammered.

"It would be amazing if it were," Rolf said. "I mean, can you imagine? A real, live griffin? But Mother, think about it: if a griffin had hatched in the Castle in the last hundred years, wouldn't we all know about it?"

"That's true," Queen Celina admitted.

Despite her mother's slightly downcast expression, Celie sagged with relief. She silently thanked Rolf for coming to her rescue, even if he didn't know that he had. Hoping that no one would notice, she started backing toward the door of the tower. She wanted to get to her room and start reading the new book in earnest, almost as much as she wanted to get away from Arkwright before he somehow connected her to the shards of orange shell in the hatching tower.

But when she got to her bedchamber, all was quiet. A quick look told her that Rufus wasn't there. She put her book and satchel on the table under the windows and went up to his tower.

He wasn't in the tower, either.

One of the shutters was unlatched, and cold air was blowing into the room. Celie ran to the open window and looked down. Below her was the main courtyard. There was no sign of Rufus. A guard walked across it, unhurried, and then a pair of councilors, their heads together as they talked. None of them showed any indication that a griffin had just swooped overhead.

Celie started to close the shutter, then changed her mind and left it wide open, in case Rufus came back that way. She didn't know where to go next or how to look for him. She supposed he could have unlatched the shutter and then gone downstairs and out the door of Celie's bedchamber, but she doubted it. And if he had flown, he could be anywhere. On one of the Castle's many roofs, out in the sheep meadow, in the village . . . beyond the village and halfway to Sleyne City . . .

She turned to run out of the tower, but stopped when she saw Flat Squirrel on the floor. She scooped it up and wrapped it around her left arm like a fur muff. On her way out of her bedroom she grabbed up her cloak, grateful that she had taken the time to put on Rufus's harness before she went to her lessons.

Out in the courtyard she looked around. Everyone was going about their usual business, and she knew that they wouldn't have been if they'd seen something the size of Rufus flying overhead. The sunlight was pale, but he would still have cast a rather large shadow. She turned and went around the side of the Castle. The tower windows looked out over the courtyard on one side and the stables on the other.

Hoping against hope, she headed for the stables. The grooms looked at her curiously as she walked through the warm, straw- and horse-scented room. She swept her hand along the soft noses of a few curious horses who hung their heads over the stall doors, but she kept moving. She needed to find Rufus before someone else did.

Through the stable and around to the new stable. As soon as she walked through the door she heard Rufus give a cry of welcome, and Celie furiously hugged him. He caught sight of Flat Squirrel and tried to pull away, but she wrapped a hand in one of his harness handles and shook the hated toy in his face.

"You are so naughty! Don't ever do that again!"

She heard the scrape of a boot at the door, and tried to shove Rufus into a stall.

"It's just me," Pogue called out. "I saw you run out the door with Flat Squirrel on your arm and thought you might need a little help."

"What am I going to do with him?" Celie wailed to Pogue as he came down the aisle.

"I don't know," Pogue said. He stood in front of them, arms folded, and rocked back and forth on his heels. "I just don't know. I don't understand what the Castle is doing at all. Most of the court has now traipsed through the tower where he hatched and fingered the pieces of shell there. And he just flew in broad daylight, didn't he? Do you think it's time to show him to the king and queen?"

"I'd like to," Celie began, doubtful.

As if in answer, the door to the stable blew shut.

"See!" She pointed to it. "That happens every time!"

"That was the wind," Pogue said.

"It wasn't," Celie insisted. "I felt that funny twist in my brain."

"What?"

"When the Castle does something, I feel a funny little twisting inside my head, like a headache is going to start but doesn't." Celie had only recently figured out the connection.

Pogue looked at her in astonishment. "I've never felt anything like that," he said, and she thought she detected envy in his voice.

"Perhaps it's just a Glower family thing," Celie mumbled, embarrassed. "But I just started noticing it, since the Castle's been going crazy."

"I'll have to ask Bran if he gets it, too," Pogue said. "But anyway, we've got to get Rufus back inside the Castle somehow, and apparently you're still not allowed to just walk him right out of here." He sighed.

"I guess he'll have to fly back," Celie said. "Thank goodness it's starting to get dark out."

"Plus your cloak is dark blue," Pogue said, coming closer. He cupped his hands like he was going to help her mount a horse. "That will help a bit."

"What are you doing?" Now it was Celie's turn to stare in astonishment.

"Do you honestly trust him to fly straight back to his tower?" Pogue raised one eyebrow. "You're going to have to ride him back, and guide him."

"Absolutely not!" Bran had come into the stable, and

now he slammed the door shut behind him, glaring at them both. "Are you mad?"

"We can't walk through the doors of the Castle with a griffin," Celie said, warming to Pogue's idea. After all, Rufus was wearing a harness. And he'd clearly gotten the hang of flying. She pointed out these things to Bran.

"When did you cook up this little plan, Pogue?" Bran frowned at his friend, as though Pogue were deliberately leading Celie astray.

Pogue began to argue with Bran, telling him how the Castle had slammed the door at the very mention of revealing Rufus, and using the tapestry cushions as proof that it could be done. Meanwhile, Celie put her knee into Pogue's cupped hands, and he boosted her easily onto Rufus's back. She sat up straight while Rufus shifted under her and tried to look poised, as though she rode griffins all the time. The truth was that she hardly even rode her pony anymore, and Rufus was not as much like a pony as she'd thought.

His back was narrower than her pony's, and bonier, and the muscles that moved his wings rolled under his hide in a way that made her feel like he could slide her right onto his rump and then to the floor if she didn't hold on carefully. She wrapped her legs around his middle, tugging up her skirts and wishing that she were wearing her divided riding skirt, though she'd hardly thought she would be riding Rufus when she left her rooms earlier.

"It's all right, Bran," Celie said. "Let's just do this and get it over with."

"It doesn't need to be gotten over with," Bran protested.

"The Castle wants me to raise this griffin properly," she said, though really she didn't know how far the Castle wanted her to take Rufus's training. "And he needs to be trained to carry a rider. You've seen the tapestries: griffins are being ridden in them!"

"I'll fix your cloak," Pogue said, adjusting the fabric to cover as much of Rufus as possible. "Sorry, Bran. I'm not trying to pick a fight with you, or endanger your little sister. But if we're going to do this, we need to do it fast. The guards will check in here when they come on evening duty."

"Bran, can you make us invisible?" Celie asked.

"No," Bran said sourly. "It takes far too much preparation, and it wears off too quickly. And if I could make Rufus invisible, I would insist that we walk him into the Castle anyway." He sighed heavily.

Celie's heart rose. "So you're going to let me fly with him?"

"I don't see how I can stop you," Bran said. He rubbed his face with both hands.

"Thank you," Celie said. "Now . . . how do I get him to walk?"

But as soon as the word "walk" left her mouth, Rufus moved forward. Celie grabbed for the handles. They were located just in front of the widest, most saddle-like part of the harness, which meant that her hands were gripping just in front of her thighs, with her skirts tangled around them. Her legs were hanging down in front of Rufus's wings, which made it very hard to squeeze with her knees the way she would on her pony. But still, she managed to find her balance as he went toward the door of the stable. To her relief, he moved so smoothly that it felt as if he were flowing like water rather than walking, all of his usual awkwardness gone. It made staying in place easier than she'd feared.

At the door, Rufus came to a halt. Bran stepped around him and peered out the door, looking carefully into the growing darkness.

"It's clear," he whispered. "And thank the powers it gets dark so early in the winter. Go now! Hurry!"

Celie took her hands off the harness just long enough to pull up the hood of her cloak. Hood in place, she grabbed the harness handles again and leaned close along Rufus's neck.

"Rufus," she said in a low, commanding voice, "fly up to the tower! Fly!" She clucked her tongue.

Rufus didn't move.

Bran started to say something, but Celie shook her head frantically. Rufus wasn't moving, but that was because he'd gone very still when she told him to fly. Every muscle that she could feel beneath her had locked into place, and his head was no longer moving from side to side as it usually did while he took in his surroundings.

"Rufus, fly," she whispered.

So suddenly that it took her breath away, Rufus launched himself into the air.

Celie's stomach stayed on the ground. She screamed, but the wind took her scream away. Her hands slicked with sweat, and she had to shove them under the harness itself to stay on his back. Rufus shot into the sky like an arrow, and Celie wondered when he would stop. Could they actually touch the clouds? The thought exhilarated and frightened her at the same time.

High above the Castle, Rufus snapped his wings out wide like sails, and they stopped moving upward. He circled in the cold air, Celie clinging to his back, laughing and crying at the wonder of it all. Below them were the lights of the Castle, beyond the high outer wall she could see the glowing windows of the village, and far above them the stars appeared like gleaming chips of ice.

She was trembling all over from nerves and cold. The air above the Castle was even more frigid than that near the ground, and when Rufus flapped his wings it funneled more cold air around her. She had to lean in close to his neck to keep the wind from tearing her off his back, which gave her the added benefit of feeling the warmth from his neck on her cheeks.

"Take us to the tower, Rufus," she called to him.

The force of their upward flight had ripped the hood back off her hair, and she knew he could hear her. He clacked his beak in reply, but then he swooped around the Spyglass Tower and kept on until they were over the sheep meadow. She pulled at the harness, trying to find a way to guide him.

"Rufus! Take us to the tower at once," she ordered. "The tower with your toys in it. And food. Food, Rufus!"

He wheeled, and Celie had to clamp down with her legs to keep from toppling off his shoulder. But then he flew past the Castle in the opposite direction, taking them over the village. They were lower than before, and Celie was afraid that someone would spot them, despite the increasing darkness.

"Rufus! Take us home!"

The griffin tilted back his head and let out a scream. But then he angled his wings and swung around. With only a few flaps he brought them back to the Castle. He circled around the Spyglass Tower again, and then the hatching tower, before aiming for the new tower that rose above Celie's bedchamber. She was grateful all over again for whatever magic kept the other residents of the Castle from seeing that slender structure, jutting out at the very front of the Castle. Then she had another worry: the windows were far narrower than Rufus's wings.

At the last possible second, he folded his wings in and they half flew, half fell into the tower. Celie was thrown from Rufus's back, tumbling over and over on the rush matting to land in a tangle at Bran's feet. Rufus skidded a little ways, crashing into Pogue, who fell on his backside with an oath.

"Celie! Are you all right?" Bran rushed over to help her up.

"Oh," she said, feeling dazed. "Good, you all made it up here."

"This was a mistake," Bran said, straightening his wizardly robes. "You could have been killed."

"You flew," Pogue said. He was taking the harness off Rufus, grinning. "How was it?"

"It was wonderful," Celie told him. "And I'm going again tomorrow night!"

Chapter 20

Celie woke up still buzzing with excitement over the events of the previous day. But her excitement was short-lived. Master Humphries had decided that he would die of shame if, as well as being fluent in Grathian, the three younger Glower children didn't know the name of every Grathian king since Grath was founded, and be able to greet the ambassadors from Larien and Bendeswe in their own languages.

The court was still in an uproar over the queen's discovery of the hatching tower, but all Celie wanted was some peace and quiet so that she could read the book Lulath had given her until darkness fell, and she and Rufus could take off once again.

Lulath's book was a miracle. The author, Wizard Hadlocke, was not only notable for having been a woman, but also happened to have been Celie's many-times-great-grandmother. And she had had a passion for uncovering the Castle's secrets that rivaled Celie and Bran's.

Wizard Hadlocke had scoured the countryside, collecting stories about Castle Glower, and had written them all down with notations about what elements of the story were true and what were exaggerated or couldn't be verified.

She also recorded the story Celie had heard about Castle Glower appearing suddenly one day, though her language was considerably more poetic. Hadlocke described the griffins "swarming out of the Castle to hunt the gleaming unicorms," and said that "Larien's bold king, moved to tears of sorrow, did send ships for the shining beasts to convey them on their final journey." Celie could not tell if "final journey" was a nice way of saying they died, or if it meant climbing the rainbows to some magical realm.

More fascinating even than that was talk of the people who had come with the Castle. Hadlocke called them survivors, and mentioned wounds that killed some of them after the Castle's appearance, but Celie couldn't tell whether the wounds were from a battle or some sort of plague. There were references to both, and Hadlocke was frustratingly vague on that point.

Rolf had joined her after their lessons, and soon read through the bestiary and the epic poetry, and even found the poems of Karksus that Arkwright had recommended, but hadn't found anything half as interesting. The bestiary had merely stated that griffins were half eagle and half lion, and probably mythical. The accompanying illustration had been quite rough, and Rolf had said with disgust that he could have done a better job himself. The poem that Celie had copied for Master Humphries had contained the only mention of griffins in that book, and the Karksus poetry was so dense and dramatic that even Celie thought the author was probably being fanciful.

"So, apparently griffins were ridden by giants who threw balls of fire at their enemies and cracked the earth with their war cries," Rolf reported, tossing the volume of Karksus down on a table in the holiday feasting hall. "But they would lie down and die of ennui if there weren't any battles happening."

"What's 'on-wee'?" Celie asked as she lovingly turned the pages of Hadlocke's book and showed Rolf a much more skilled drawing of a griffin.

"Ennui is, basically, boredom. The mighty griffin riders, fierce of eye, noble in battle, bold in love, would get *bored* and die," Rolf said, rolling his eyes. "I think Karksus had read too many of those unicorn stories Lilah used to like, and decided to try it with griffins."

"Well, Hadlocke says that the griffin riders were dying when they arrived in Sleyne," Celie told him. "So maybe Karksus really did know some of them, and thought they were dying of ennui because they were already sick."

"Hadlocke . . . Hathelocke . . . ," Rolf said. "Do you think this great-great-grandmother of ours was related to the fearsome Hathelockes?"

"No," Celie said. "The Hathelockes conquered some land called the Glorious Arkower. And I'm not sure they were entirely human."

"So do you think Hadlocke's book is real?" Rolf asked seriously. "Do you think the Castle just appeared one day, spilled out a bunch of griffins and sickly giants, and then . . . what?"

"I guess the griffin riders all died," Celie said. She cleared her throat a little. To her surprise, thinking of the strange, noble people of the tapestries all dying had made her choke up a little. "And the griffins died soon after."

She'd just found that part, and turned the pages to show Rolf, not trusting her voice. Griffins bonded to their riders at hatching, and rarely outlived them. Likewise, a rider whose griffin was killed often sickened and died even if he hadn't been wounded. She supposed that might look like ennui to an outsider, but she couldn't imagine life without Rufus, even though he'd only hatched a couple of months ago. Her whole day revolved around him, despite the fact that no one but Bran and Pogue knew he existed.

"If I only believed Karksus, I'd be convinced that griffins weren't real and never had been," Rolf said. He patted the cover of Hadlocke's book. "But the amount of detail you've shown me in this book makes me think they could be. It's so matter-of-fact: This is the day the griffins came.

This is what they looked like. This is how they lived. This is how they died."

"Who died?"

Wizard Arkwright was standing in the archway of the hall.

"No one," Celie and Rolf said in chorus.

Arkwright raised one of his eyebrows. Celie was struck anew by how much he looked like the griffin riders on the tapestry, and like some of her ancestors from the portrait gallery as well. Really, his eyebrows were freakishly mobile, and his forehead was much too high to be normal.

His eyes lit on the books on the table. "I see you found the Karksus I recommended," he said. He came over to the table and picked the book up, smoothing his hands over the cover. "What do you think of him?"

"Honestly?" Rolf shrugged. "A bit elaborate for my taste."

"He felt very passionately about the griffins and their masters," Arkwright said. "And it's written in a style that has never been the fashion in Sleyne."

"Yeah, the verses are a little weird," Rolf said.

"Well, he wasn't writing in Sleynth," Arkwright said defensively.

"Was he Grathian?" Celie asked.

"No" was all Arkwright said.

He put the book down, and then saw Hadlocke's book. Celie watched him start, and then she noticed that his hands had begun to shake.

"Where did you find this?"

"Prince Lulath gave it to me," Celie said.

She resisted the urge to leap forward and snatch the book away from Arkwright. He didn't try to pick it up, though—he just touched it with trembling fingertips, as though he were afraid it would sting him.

"Lulath? How did he . . ."

"It belonged to one of his ancestors," Rolf said. He had one eyebrow raised, though not as far as Arkwright's had been. "But he gifted it to the Castle, and to Celie and me specifically, when he realized that it was a history of Castle Glower."

"It does not belong here," Arkwright began. "It belongs . . ." He trailed off.

"Where?" Celie asked when he didn't continue.

"I do wish you wouldn't store such things here," Arkwright complained. "It's not wise."

"Why not?"

Arkwright wheeled around. His face was white and strained, and it looked even less human than the tapestry people now.

"It simply isn't, you foolish little girl. You have no idea what you're toying with!"

"Get a grip on yourself, man!" Rolf stood up and faced Arkwright. "You're a guest in the Castle, and if you don't watch yourself, you'll find your invitation revoked by the Castle itself."

Arkwright started laughing. "The Castle could no more rid itself of me than I of it," he said. "But if you continue to play with matters you cannot understand, you might find your own 'invitation revoked,'" he said. Then he turned and stalked out of the feasting hall.

"That was weird," Rolf said when the sound of Arkwright's angry steps had faded away.

"Yes, yes, it was," Celie said. With surprise she found that she was shaking so hard that her teeth chattered when she spoke.

"Let me take you to your room, Cel," he said.

"No!" She said it a little too vehemently, and Rolf gave her an even more concerned look. "I just . . . I've never gotten a good look at the new map room."

"Oh, really? It's quite something," Rolf said. "Follow me."

He took her upstairs to a room that was basically the twin of the fabric room, except instead of bolt after bolt of fabric, spools of lace and ribbon, and tables scarred by large steel shears, there was rack after rack of rolled maps and high desks to lay them on. Some of the maps weren't drawn on parchment, either, but were carved into wood, or burned on leather, or etched on silver.

The royal cartographer was there, working at a high, slanted desk. He looked up when they came in, an irritated expression on his face at being interrupted. But when he saw that it was Celie, he smiled.

"Ah! Your Highnesses! Is there anything I can do for you?"

"No," Celie said. "I was just looking for a quiet place to study, and realized that I'd never seen this room."

"I said I'd show her," Rolf said. "We don't want to bother you, though."

"Not at all," the royal cartographer said cheerfully. "Let me show you some wonderful things."

He took them around the room and showed them scrolls of maps that had been done in wonderful rich colors. He showed them a map made of wood and clay on a tray that depicted the entire valley. The two etched silver maps were of the stars, though one of them showed constellations that Celie had never heard of before.

"Is this the southern sky?" Celie asked, looking at the strange star map.

"No," the royal cartographer said. "These are no stars we've ever seen before. Even the Royal Wizard cannot identify them.

"But most of these maps are of places no one has ever seen," he said, gesturing around the room with a broad sweep of his arm. "Cities that exist only in legend, or have never existed at all. Ranges of mountains drawn from the artist's fancy, countries that could not possibly be real."

"You don't think so?"

Celie had lived all her life in magical Castle Glower, and had hatched and raised a griffin. She could imagine quite a lot of things that "could not be real" being real.

“I’ve traveled all over the world,” the cartographer said, matter-of-fact. “I’ve never seen mountain ranges like this, lakes this vast.” He tapped one of the scrolls. “But would you like to see my favorite of these fictional maps?”

Celie and Rolf both nodded eagerly.

The cartographer took a heavy, round platter from one of the shelves and set it on the largest table. Rolf and Celie crowded around to look, and discovered that it wasn’t a platter. It was a circular map made of beautifully inlaid exotic woods.

It depicted a country covered in forest, with a large lake in the northern part bordered by mountains. The trees of the forest were made of a wood that was greenish in color, and the lake was silvery gray. The mountains were a rich, dark wood that was nearly black, and the plains to the south were smooth caramel brown.

“I’ve never seen wood like this,” Rolf said, running a reverent finger over the green wood. “It’s like satin.”

“I’ve never seen most of these woods,” the cartographer confided. “Nor any country like this. Judging from the scale of the mountains and trees, this lake is enormous. And look at this,” he said, pointing to an emblem at the top of the map. “It’s worn, but do you see what this is?”

“A griffin,” Celie breathed.

In the blank space at the top of the map, above the border of the strange land, a griffin made of golden wood had been carefully inlaid. Time had faded its color, and many hands had worn it so smooth that Celie hadn’t noticed it until the cartographer pointed it out. The map reminded her of something, but she couldn't put her finger on what it was that seemed so familiar.

"Could we take this down to the holiday feasting hall?" Rolf brushed a finger over the griffin.

Celie thought that the cartographer was going to object, but after a moment's hesitation, he said, "As Your Highnesses wish. No one else is using it."

"You can come and look at it as often as you like," Celie offered. "It's just that we're doing a project for our brother, Bran, and gathering up all the things we find that have pictures or stories about griffins and putting them in one place to study."

"That reminds me," Rolf said. "You've traveled a lot; have you ever found anything in your travels about griffins? Other maps featuring them? Statues? Heard any interesting stories?"

The cartographer frowned, and thought for a while. "No," he said after a minute. "I never have. There's the flag, of course, but that's all. There are no griffins anywhere else in Sleyne."

The cartographer helped Rolf carry the wooden map down to the holiday feasting hall, where Celie was relieved to find no sign of Arkwright. The cartographer looked at their collection with bemusement, then excused himself to go back to the map room.

Rolf put an arm around Celie, concerned. He helped her carry the Hadlocke book back to her room, just in case

Arkwright decided to steal it in the night. Celie was so distracted by the encounter with Arkwright and then the revelation of the wooden map that she almost couldn't go flying with Rufus that night.

Almost.

Chapter 21

Flying with Rufus was Celie's greatest joy.

Three nights in a row now she had gone out, circling the towers and swooping over the fields surrounding the Castle, clinging to Rufus in terrified delight. Pogue had had to rig some extra straps across the chest and back of the harness to hold it in place, and Celie had yet to dare lying along Rufus's back. But she had started wearing her riding dress for convenience, with a thick, dark scarf wrapped around her head to ward off the chill of the air. A cloak was useless with the wind blowing the hood back, and the body of the cape streaming out behind her made her feel conspicuous.

Rufus's landings were getting better, and so were his beginning jumps. Celie no longer felt like he was going to shoot her straight at the moon, or knock her silly by rolling her across the floor and into the stone walls headfirst when they returned to the tower. Impressed by his rapid progress, they had all agreed to try him with another rider, namely Bran, who was the tallest of the three of them but more slender than Pogue, and a wizard besides.

Rufus, however, was having none of it.

To say that he was balking was putting it mildly. He was backed against a wall, hissing, tail lashing, and occasionally swiping at their ankles with his eagle-like foreclaws. Bran was trying to win him over with a biscuit while he talked softly and steadily about what a fine, fine griffin Rufus was. Celie was telling Rufus over and over what a lovely person Bran was, and Pogue had Flat Squirrel and was threatening to tie it to Rufus's harness so that he could never shake it off.

"I think this is a bad idea," Bran said finally. "He doesn't want me on his back, and that's that. I'd hate to force him to carry me and have him shake me off a hundred paces in the air."

"Well, I think it's very bad of you, Rufus," Celie said, even though she was secretly glad.

"Do you think he imprinted on Celie, like a duck on its mother?" Pogue said.

Bran nodded, tossing the biscuit. "It's all yours, Rufus."

The griffin dived for the treat, flipping it into his beak with one claw and swallowing it whole. Then he snuffled around the floor and, eventually, Bran, looking for more.

"Of course I'm his mother," Celie said. She'd almost said "rider," thinking of the books she'd been reading, but stopped herself. She didn't feel ready to talk about that yet. It was too strange and wonderful to put herself in the same category as those warriors of legend. "I've taken care of him since the moment he was hatched," she went on. "I don't see any other person or griffin here who can say the same." She felt her ears turn red when she heard how that probably sounded. "Not that you all haven't helped a great deal, and I'm very grateful," she hastened to add.

"No," Bran said, waving a hand, "it's true. He's definitely bonded to you." He smiled ruefully.

"Do you think that the Castle might bring out another egg sometime?" Pogue asked.

"I can't imagine anything more horrible," Bran said. "If it does, I'm going to be very careful not to be there when it hatches."

"I might like to hatch one," Pogue said.

Celie fought down another stab of jealousy. She would love to be the one who hatched another egg. She wanted all the eggs . . . to be known as the only person in the world who knew how to raise and train a griffin! But realistically, she knew that she could only handle Rufus with the help of Bran, Pogue, and the Castle. More griffins would be far too much.

"We'll have to tell Mother and Father if there is another egg," she said with a laugh. "I don't think we could hide two griffins!"

The others didn't laugh, and no one said anything else for a moment. The unspoken thought they shared was that they wouldn't be able to hide Rufus in this tower forever, even though there was only one of him. Once he reached his adult size, it would be like hiding a warhorse in Celie's bedroom.

Rufus, having thoroughly searched the room and Bran for any more treats, now came to Celie and made pleading noises. He rubbed himself against her and then turned so that his back was to her, lowering one wing to make it easier for her to climb on.

"Oh, did you want to go flying, Rufus?" She feigned surprise.

He gave her an irritated look over his shoulder.

Celie laughed and eagerly climbed onto his back.

Once she was in place, Rufus scuttled over to the window that they had left open. Celie looked back at her brother and Pogue.

"You don't have to wait here all night for me, you know," she told them. "We'll be fine!" She didn't add that there was nothing they could do to help her if something did go wrong while she and Rufus were flying over the valley.

"Do you really think I could sleep while my little sister is up in the air on the back of a half-grown, half-trained griffin?" Bran made a face.

"I second that," Pogue said, "even though you're not my sister. Knowing you're out there all the same . . ."

Bran gave a grim bark of laughter, but Celie was too busy holding Rufus in check. His front claws were gripping the scarred windowsill, and every line of his body was taut. She stroked his neck.

"Let's go," she whispered.

He leaped into the sky.

They flew. They soared. They wheeled and glided. It was like an elaborate dance through the air. The cold wind teased at them and they danced with it, turning and tasting it, letting it push them and then twirling away from its grasp. Celie was more alive on Rufus's back than she was even in the Castle, making her maps. She and Rufus belonged together, and they belonged in the sky. She felt pity for Bran and Pogue who, it seemed, would never know this joy unless the Castle gave them griffins of their own.

They raced over the sheep meadow, then beyond to the village fields that lay still and frozen, the moon glinting off odd patches of leftover snow. Rufus flew almost to the trees at the far end of the valley before Celie tugged at the left handle of the harness, turning him. He was much more responsive to her commands now, and she had stopped threatening him with a bridle and reins. Not that there would be any way to rig a bridle for a griffin. His head was too round and sleek, and his beak could bite through sticks as thick as Celie's wrist; she doubted that a bit would last long.

The Castle was tightly shuttered, and Celie figured that everyone had long since gone to bed. So she let Rufus play among the towers, swooping close around them and turning so that he stood almost sideways in the air. She suppressed a loud whoop of joy.

As they glided past the windows of the Spyglass Tower, which had no shutters, Celie thought she saw a faint glimmer of light. She turned toward it, and Rufus turned with her. She could see by the way his head was cocked that he'd seen the light as well. They made a circle of the shadowy tower. As they finished their circuit, one of the shadows moved.

Celie hauled back on the handles, causing Rufus to go lower, twisting away from the tower. She looked back as they fled, and saw someone leaning out of the tower with a hooded lamp in their hand, so that only the faintest slit of light showed.

She leaned along Rufus's neck. "Back to your tower, boy, go back!"

Rufus beat his wings in a frantic rhythm, sensing her fear. They lunged through the window of Rufus's tower, startling Bran and Pogue, who leaped to their feet, each of them tossing down a notebook.

"What is it?"

Bran ran forward and helped Celie get off Rufus's back. Rufus's wings were still half-extended, and he was clacking his beak and making shrill sounds. Pogue put his big hands on the griffin's head and stroked him, whispering soothingly.

"Someone saw you, didn't they?" Pogue's face was pale under his tan.

"They were in the Spyglass Tower," Celie said with a gasp.

"Maybe it was the moon reflecting off a spyglass," Bran said, but he sounded doubtful.

Celie knew what she'd seen. "Arkwright," she said in despair. "It was Arkwright."

"Are you sure?"

"He had a lantern with a hood on it," she said, slumping to the ground. Bran sat beside her, and Rufus flopped down with his head in her lap. "I saw a glimmer of light in the tower, so we flew around it, and I saw something move. Rufus dropped down, and when I looked back someone was leaning out with the lantern. He was tall, with a thin, pale face . . ."

"Arkwright," Pogue said, his mouth a tight line. "What do we do?"

"We do nothing," Bran said. "He'll have to find this tower to find Rufus, and I don't think the Castle will allow that. If he says anything, just play dumb. Rolf told Father about him threatening you today; Father and Mother are both very angry. If Father could toss Arkwright out of the Castle on his rear end, he would. But the College would never stand for it, so we all have to pretend we aren't bothered."

"Just like we did with Khelsh," Pogue said. "It will drive him insane if we pretend that he's beneath our notice, or that we know something he doesn't."

"All right," Celie said, stroking Rufus's feathers. They were still stiff and cold from the air outside. "But I think I like this even less than I liked toying with Khelsh."

"That's because Khelsh just plotted and shouted," Pogue said. "Arkwright seems to be always on the verge of turning us all into flies and then swatting us."

"Don't worry," Bran said with a faint smile. "That sort of magic is beyond even him."

"How reassuring," Celie said dryly.

Chapter 22

The next day was Tuesday. When Celie entered the winter dining hall for breakfast, she found the table covered in maps, and Bran was explaining to the family that all Pogue's earlier predictions about the Castle had come true. The corridors and rooms he'd told them about had appeared, splitting the Castle into two distinct sections. But he hadn't foreseen the large barracks that were now behind the griffin stable, which cut through the back wall surrounding the Castle. It was worse than the break caused by the new stables. The wall looked like it had been hit by a battering ram: stones and chunks of mortar were scattered all across the sheep meadow, and it was fortunate that the sheep had still been in their barn when it happened, or they surely would have been killed.

King Glower summoned the entire court to the throne

room, the Glower family trailing after. Celie and Lilah were wearing two of their new gowns, made from fabric the castle had provided: matching blue velvet that hung in heavy, rich folds.

Lilah had altered one of the ancient patterns that had been found in the fabric room, and had a stiff, rectangular cape hanging down from her shoulders. It was made from satin that had a random pattern of triangles and a large circle embroidered on it. It almost made a picture, but the embroidery was subtle enough that you couldn't quite make out what it was a picture of.

Celie liked that the thick fabric of her own gown made her feel safe and warm. She almost wished she had a cape as well, but didn't want to be too weighed down. Something bad was happening to the Castle, she could feel it. She smoothed her skirt and listened to her father.

"Friends," King Glower said, his voice deep with concern. "The Castle is in crisis. Once rooms and corridors changed with a sense of whimsy, or because it filled a need for those who live here. Now the changes have become drastic and even dangerous." He sighed.

"I must warn you all to stay away from the outer wall," the king continued. "Large portions of it have been weakened by the breaks made this morning, and we are concerned that other sections may collapse. We have stonemasons working to shore it up, but until they do, please stay clear of it. Likewise, the Armor Gallery is still off limits. The Royal Wizard and Wizard Arkwright have been able to uncover the purpose of most of the weapons therein, but those they have studied haved proved to be highly dangerous.

"In the meantime, the heads of the guard, housekeeping, and cooking staff and the Council have all been issued copies of Princess Cecelia's atlas. It is as up-to-date as my daughter and the royal cartographer can make it. If you lose your way and do not have access to an atlas, just remember the two rules, which, fortunately, still hold true: keep going east and you'll find the throne room, or turn left three times and climb out a window to find the kitchens."

One of the councilors came forward, holding his hand up to ask a question.

"Yes, Lord Sefton?"

"Why is this happening?"

"We don't know yet," the king said, sighing heavily. "But we are doing our best to find out."

And with that less-than-reassuring statement, King Glower excused everyone but the family, Wizard Arkwright, Lulath, and Pogue. They all looked around at one another, at a loss.

"Is the danger of the gravest?" Lulath asked when no one else spoke.

"Bran?" The king was sitting on the throne, rubbing his face, which Celie knew meant that he was tired and frustrated.

"We don't know," Bran said. "It definitely seems bad.

Nothing in Grandfather's journal indicates that the Castle ever made changes this severe during his time here. Celie?"

Celie was already shaking her head. "There's nothing in Hadlocke's book, either."

"Hadlocke?" King Glower looked at her, then at Bran.

"Is this part of your project, dear?" Queen Celina asked.

"Yes," Celie said. "Rolf and I have been trying to find anything we could about griffins, putting it all in the holiday feasting hall. We've found cushions, tapestries—"

"An anvil," Rolf put in. "And a wooden map."

"Several books," Celie went on. "One of them is a history of the Castle written by one of the former Royal Wizards, an ancestress of ours named Hadlocke."

Wizard Arkwright made a muffled sound, like he'd been struck. Everyone looked at him, but the king signaled Celie to continue.

"We're starting to piece together the history of the Castle," Celie told her father eagerly. "And it seems that griffins are real, and that they once lived here in the Castle with their riders!"

"That is indeed strange and wonderful news," her father said patiently. "But I'm afraid it doesn't explain what's happening here and now to the Castle."

"It does," Bran said, and Celie shot him a warning glance. He ignored her. "It tells us a great deal. There once were griffins and riders in this Castle when it stood in another land, but then the Castle came here, to Sleyne, and now they're gone. I suspect, from what Celie has told me of her studies, that the Castle brought parts of itself here for self-defense. It brought griffins and warriors, too, but they were dying and didn't live long. Now I think it's bringing more and more rooms here, and keeping them here, because it's being threatened again."

"You mean, back . . . wherever the rest of it is?" King Glower's face was pale.

"Exactly," Bran said, nodding.

Celie was aghast. The Castle was in danger? Was that why it had brought Rufus's egg here? Who was attacking? Was there anything they could do to help?

"What can we do?" King Glower asked, echoing Celie's thoughts.

"I don't know," Bran admitted.

"If I may interject?" Wizard Arkwright looked at the king, his eyebrows raised.

"By all means, sir," King Glower said. "If you know anything, or can help in any way . . ."

Wizard Arkwright gave a curt nod. "Your Majesty, I have studied the Castle all my life," he began.

Bran frowned, and so did Celie. If this was the case, then why had he never been there? How had Celie, or her father, never heard of him until he appeared in the courtyard?

"And I can assure you," Wizard Arkwright went on, "that the Castle is not under attack. It is not threatened—it is angry. Angry because something very precious has been stolen from it."

"Stolen?" Bran and King Glower said at the same time.

"Who would dare to steal from Castle Glower?" The king looked more bemused than anything else. "And what did they steal?"

"A griffin."

"That *was* a griffin's egg that I found, wasn't it?" Queen Celina stood up, moving back and forth restlessly in front of her throne. "Where is the griffin that hatched from it? Do you know, Arkwright? Who stole it?"

The wizard sighed heavily. Then he turned and looked straight at Celie. She realized she had been so distracted by his eloquent eyebrows that she had never looked at the color of his eyes before. They were a pale golden-brown that reminded her of Rufus's eyes.

"I'm sorry, Princess Cecelia. But you must give back the griffin. It doesn't belong here."

Celie's mouth went dry. She couldn't move. She couldn't talk. She just stared into Arkwright's strange golden eyes.

"What?" King Glower leaped to his feet. "Impossible! Celie couldn't have stolen a griffin; where would she hide it?"

"Princess Cecelia," Arkwright said, "tell us where you're hiding the griffin. It has to go back."

"Of course it has to go back," King Glower said. "But it can't have been Celie who stole it." He turned to Bran. "Can you do some magic to locate it, or shall we bring in the soldiers to search?"

Celie's gaze was still held by Arkwright. They were

facing each other across the throne room. Celie didn't know what to do. Her legs were starting to shake and her feet and hands felt numb. He knew. He had seen her and Rufus, flying together. He knew that was the real reason she was collecting the things in the holiday feasting hall. But she hadn't stolen Rufus, she hadn't!

"Just run," Pogue muttered.

"What?" Celie flinched. She'd forgotten anyone else was in the room. Even her father's increasingly heated voice and Bran's low murmur had faded. All she could see was Arkwright's eyes.

"Give me the griffin, princess," Arkwright said.

"Celie," Queen Celina said.

Celie managed to move. She turned her head to look at her mother.

"May I see it?" Her mother's voice was soft, her eyes wide with amazement. The question stopped King Glower, and Bran, and then everyone was looking at Celie.

"It's not some prize-winning pig to be gawked at and stroked for luck," Arkwright said. "It has to go back to the Glorious Arkower where it belongs! At once!"

Chapter 23

Celie didn't need Pogue's finger to jab her in the back, or to hear his soft curse. The look on Arkwright's face was enough to urge her to run. She burst through the throne room doors and was across the main hall and in her room before anyone could react or begin pursuit.

In her room she locked the door and then dragged a heavy chair in front of it. She knew it wouldn't stop a wizard, but at least it would buy them some time. She grabbed her heavy wool cloak from its hook and ran up the stairs to Rufus's tower. She prayed that this one time she would find him, and not learn that he had gotten loose again and was now happily chewing Wizard Arkwright's shoes.

But no—he was there, eating parched corn from his dish. He gave a glad cry when he saw Celie, and ran toward her. She sent up another silent prayer, this one of thanks that, once again, she'd remembered to put on his harness after she fed him breakfast.

She fastened her cloak at her throat, shoved Flat Squirrel in the back of her sash where Rufus couldn't see it, and undid one of the shutters. Rufus watched her with his head tilted to one side, clearly baffled by her rapid, jerky movements and the fact that she seemed to want to go flying in broad daylight. She actually had to cluck her tongue and coax him over to the window.

"Come here, Rufus! Come here, boy! Let's go flying!"

She could hear someone pounding on her bedroom door, far below the tower room. Rufus heard it, too, and started to turn away from her. His wings were rising up above him like a shield, a sure sign that he was becoming agitated.

"Rufus! Don't you want to go flying?"

The griffin turned back, unable to resist the call of the open window.

"Good boy," Celie said, trying to keep the panic out of her words.

She grabbed the harness handles and heaved herself onto his back. He was now significantly taller than her old pony, though still narrower and bonier. She gripped both handles tight and squeezed his ribs with her knees.

"Let's go!"

With a lunge and a swoop that nearly left Celie's stomach behind, the girl and her griffin were out the window and into the air above the Castle's main hall in seconds. Rufus hovered for a moment, and Celie steered him toward the Spyglass Tower. She didn't know where they would go after that; she just wanted to get Rufus out of the way. She'd never dreamed of leaving the Castle, leaving her family, but if Rufus was in danger . . .

She let him circle over the roofs of the Castle for a little while. They couldn't see anything—at least, not of the people inside. But Celie noticed immediately that the Castle, which used to look like such a random collection of great rooms and towers and passages, actually seemed to have a pattern now.

There were six tall towers, evenly spaced. Two very large angular roofs at the front over what she knew were the main hall and throne room, and two at the back that she thought were the summer and winter dining halls. She could see the wide, slightly flattened roof of the holiday feasting hall right in the middle, and the rest of the Castle was evenly distributed around it.

"This is amazing," she said to Rufus.

He squawked in reply.

When she guided him toward the Spyglass Tower, she saw that someone was there, hanging out a window. She started to pull on the harness to have Rufus fly away, but then she saw that it was Rolf. He was waving his arms at her, making broad gestures to try to get her and Rufus to come to the tower. With a sigh, she let Rufus fly toward her brother. If Rolf could help her, maybe bring her some food for the journey, she and Rufus had a better chance of getting . . . somewhere safe.

"You have a griffin?" Rolf shouted the question as soon as they got close. "Why didn't you tell me?"

"Look out," Celie called to him instead of answering.

Rufus still had a little trouble landing, and there was the large brass spyglass mounted on the windowsill to contend with as well. Rolf leaped out of the way just as Rufus tucked up his long legs, folded his wings, and shot through the window to land awkwardly against the large table in the middle of the tower.

He let out a squeal of pain, and Celie jumped off his back to make sure he was all right. He had probably bruised his left shoulder, but there was not much she could do about it, so she just stroked his head until he calmed down.

"A griffin," Rolf kept saying over and over. "A griffin! How . . . why . . . how long have you had a griffin?"

"Since he hatched. He's three months old," she said absently. She was looking around to see if any of the hard biscuits were left.

"Why'd you hide him from everyone? I mean, except Pogue and Bran." Rolf's voice was tinged with envy. "If you're going to let *Pogue Parry* know, then why not me?"

"You were in my room when Rufus was kicking up a fuss in his tower," she said. "But you couldn't hear him. We took that to mean that the Castle didn't want . . . well, wanted to keep Rufus hidden from as many people as possible. It wouldn't let me tell Mummy and Daddy. Bran and Pogue were the only ones." She sighed again and picked at Rufus's harness.

"Huh," Rolf said, looking deflated. "I wouldn't have told anyone, if you had asked me not to."

"I know," Celie assured him. "And I . . . well, I could have used more help! But the Castle—"

She stopped suddenly. There had been a funny twist at the back of her head that meant the Castle had changed something. She looked at Rolf, who ran one hand through his hair.

"Speaking of the Castle," she said.

"Sorry. Headache," Rolf said. "What about the Castle?"

"Did you feel a weird sort of twisting thing at the back of your head?"

"Yeah," Rolf told her. "I get that sometimes. Anyway, Father says—"

"Rolf, that means that the Castle just moved something around."

"It does?" Rolf looked stunned. "I never . . . noticed. I do have a lot of headaches on Tuesdays, but I thought it was just because I had to sit in the throne room listening to people complain about their taxes."

"Pogue can't feel it," Celie said. "It must be something to do with the family."

"That's amazing," Rolf said. "Not as amazing as that." He pointed to Rufus, who was preening his gold feathers. "But still amazing."

"I'm going to leave Rufus here, and we can go down," Celie said, pushing aside her worries. She'd made up her mind: she couldn't leave the Castle. "We should see what's changed, and I . . . I guess I can't run away from Arkwright forever," she admitted.

"That's what I was supposed to tell you," Rolf said, looking guilty. "But, er, it's hard to think when you're standing next to a griffin. Can I touch him?"

"Yes. What were you supposed to tell me?"

"Just a minute," Rolf said.

He held out one shaking hand to Rufus. Rufus stopped preening and looked at Rolf suspiciously. Celie nodded at Rufus to show him that Rolf was okay. Rolf very gently touched Rufus's golden shoulder. He stroked the feathers with two shaking fingers, then touched a wing, then dared to stroke Rufus's head.

"A real griffin," Rolf said reverently. "Oh, Celie, he's magnificent."

"Thank you," Celie said. She tapped Rufus's beak with two fingers, seeing that he had a look in his eye like he might bite Rolf's fingers. "But what were you up here to tell me?"

"Oh. Oh! You've got to come down," Rolf said. He continued to stroke Rufus, growing bold enough to put his whole hand on the griffin. "Father and Mother want to talk to you . . . everyone wants to talk to you. And they want to see *him*. You named him Rufus, right? After your old lion?"

"Yes," Celie said.

She gripped the harness strap by Rufus's neck. Did she really dare take him down to the throne room? What about Arkwright?

"Pogue and Bran have sworn that they won't let Arkwright lay a finger on Rufus," Rolf assured her. "They stopped Arkwright when he ran after you, and then they told everyone the whole story. So Arkwright knows you didn't steal anything; it's clear that the Castle gave the griffin to you."

"All right," Celie said, still reluctant.

"The thing is, Cel," Rolf continued, "we need to figure out what's happening now. Why did the Castle give you the egg? Why is it doing what it's doing?"

"I think it's under attack," Celie said, and surprised herself by how frighteningly right it felt to say that. "I think something's wrong back in . . . what did Arkwright call it?"

"The Glorious Arkower."

A little thrill ran through Celie. That was the name of the country the Hathelockes had conquered.

"Yes! I'm almost certain that's the country the Castle is from." Celie stopped. "Do you think that's why we call it *Glower*?"

"I don't know," Rolf said, thoughtful. "But I bet Arkwright does." His face was grim. "I think he knows a lot more about the Castle than he's saying. And I want to know why."

"Me, too," Celie decided. She looped one hand through

the harness handle. "I'll fly down to the main doors and go in that way."

"Oh," Rolf said. He gave Rufus a longing look. "All right."

"I'd love to let you fly down with us," Celie told him, feeling sorry that she couldn't give her brother a ride. Flying was her favorite thing, and she knew that Rolf would love it. "But he's not strong enough to carry two yet, and he won't let anyone but me on his back, anyway."

"If the Castle ever spits out another griffin egg . . ."

"You'll have to get in line behind Pogue and Bran," Celie said. "Well, maybe not Bran."

"Maybe I can pull rank," Rolf said with a grin. "See you down there."

"See you," Celie said.

She climbed onto Rufus's back and guided him to the window. He had to scrunch up a little to get past the spyglass, and ended up throwing himself clumsily out the window. Celie bit back a little scream, and Rolf let out a surprised yelp, but Rufus soon had his wings extended and turned his fall into a glide over the rooftops. They circled once, for the sheer joy of flying, and then Celie steered him down to the courtyard.

The guards in the courtyard scattered. One of them actually threw down his spear and ran for the front gates. Celie saw his sergeant grab him by the collar and haul him back to his post. She waved to them cheerfully as she dismounted. Then she led Rufus up the wide steps and into the Castle. The guards at the doors hurried to open them for her, bowing and staring.

"Nice pony," one of them said.

Celie looked over and saw that, despite his pallor, he was grinning. She grinned back, and he shook his head and whistled in amazement.

Inside the main hall, Queen Celina rushed at Celie, startling Rufus. The griffin backed up, squawking, then pushed forward, giving a warning hiss.

"Rufus, no!" Celie hauled back on his harness. "No, this is my mother!"

"Darling," Queen Celina cried, holding out a hand. "Why didn't you tell us?"

"Mother," Bran began.

"Oh, I know, I know!" Queen Celina cut him off. She was walking around Rufus, looking at him from all angles. "I know why you couldn't tell us, but still! And you've done wonderfully well, caring for him! Look how beautiful he is!"

Rufus clearly heard himself and his beloved mistress being praised, and he soon stopped hissing and began to coo and prance. He was showing off for the queen, and when she ran her elegant hand over his head, he didn't try to bite her.

"This is astonishing, Celie," King Glower said, coming over. "I still can't believe that you hatched and raised a griffin! All by yourself!"

"I did have help," Celie said. "Bran, and Pogue, and the

Castle, of course." But she felt like she might start cooing and prancing herself, with all the praise.

"Speaking of the Castle," Bran called out. "Celie, see if you can help us."

"What is it?"

She led Rufus over to where Bran, Pogue, Lilah, and Wizard Arkwright were standing. Once she got there, she could see why they were all milling around in confusion. She could also see what the Castle had changed. The archway into the holiday feasting hall had been bricked up. It hadn't disappeared, as it used to after the holidays. The archway was still plain to see. But there were now gray bricks completely closing off the room.

"So that's what ate all my shoes," Lilah remarked, looking at the griffin. She shook her head, then gave Rufus a smile and let him sniff her hand. "I might forgive you, if you turn out to be nice," she told him severely.

"When did that happen?" Celie asked, pointing to the blocked archway.

"Just a little bit ago," Bran said. "We were in the holiday feasting hall when the Castle spit us out into the main hall."

"It did what?"

"That's the way I'd describe it," Pogue agreed. "One minute we were standing there, looking at the books, and the next we were all out in the main hall." He rubbed his elbow. "I hit the arch on the way out. I'd only just come in with the leather cloaks that fell out of the chimney."

"The leather cloaks?"

So much had happened in the last few months that Celie had to struggle to remember what Pogue was talking about. Then the memory came: sitting in the winter dining hall with her family, opening her mouth to tell them about Rufus, and having a bundle of strange cloaks fall down the chimney into the fireplace and distract them.

"They're griffin-rider cloaks," Pogue said. "They're wearing them on the tapestry and on the cushions."

"They are?"

"Yes, but the tapestries are so faded that you have to have a keen eye to see it," Bran said. "And it makes sense: the leather is soft but very heavy, so the cloaks wouldn't blow around as much. And they're cut so that they wouldn't interfere with the griffin's wings."

Celie immediately resolved to take one of the cloaks to the seamstresses and see if they couldn't make one in her size.

"Bringing them into the holiday feasting hall, as you call it, was a foolish idea," Wizard Arkwright said, his voice cold.

"If you want to explain why, we would appreciate it," King Glower said, and didn't bother to hide his irritation. "First you accuse my daughter of theft, then you make these enigmatic statements about the cloaks. I want to know what you're not saying."

"Did I miss anything?" Rolf came running up, panting. "The Castle is huge now!" He put his hands on his knees and tried to catch his breath.

"That's because it's all here, isn't it?" Celie looked Arkwright in the eye and dared him to dodge the question. "I could see it when Rufus and I were flying overhead. Everything looks like it fits together just so. It's all here. And the holiday feasting hall is the center."

They all waited in silence for a long moment, and then Arkwright gave one stiff nod.

"We didn't call it the holiday feasting hall," he said at last. "It's the Heart of the Castle—of the Glorious Arkower. And it was the throne room, when my father was king."

Chapter 24

It was quiet enough in the main hall—just outside the Heart of the Castle, as Arkwright had just called it—to hear Rufus's tail brushing across the stones of the floor. The Glower family, plus Pogue, stood in a huddle around Wizard Arkwright, waiting for him to say more. Celie felt a little thrill of excitement, mingled with fear, run through her.

"Ah! My fluffy, silly little girls are snug into their beds now!" Lulath announced, hurrying into the hall. "It will for them be safer there, I think!" He smiled around, slightly nonplussed, sensing the tension. Then he caught sight of Rufus.

"Oh, the Celie," he said, taking a breath. "Such the magnificence!"

"Thank you," Celie said, smiling slightly as Lulath admired Rufus. But she refused to be distracted. "And now, Wizard Arkwright, explain!"

"Oh, is he doing the telling of what he knows?" Lulath turned to face Arkwright. "I have long thought he knows more than he will say that he is knowing."

"Precisely," King Glower said. "Please continue."

The king's brows were drawn down and his arms were folded in a way that almost made Celie feel sorry for Arkwright. Almost, but not quite.

"Who was your father?" Queen Celina prompted. "And when, exactly, was he the king?"

"According to our beliefs, his name must not be spoken," Arkwright said stiffly. "Because he has passed beyond. He ruled in the Castle over five hundred years ago, before it came to Sleyne."

"How is that even possible?" Rolf demanded. "If your father was alive over five hundred years ago, then you—"

"I am five hundred and fifty years old," Arkwright said.

"Impossible," King Glower said with a snort.

He looked like he was going to dismiss Arkwright as a madman. Celie's mouth was open, and she remembered to close it as Bran spoke.

"That explains a great deal," Bran said, eyeing his fellow wizard. "Like the amount of research you've been able to compile."

"Yes," Arkwright said. He sounded defeated. And although his face didn't look more than forty years old, his eyes looked every one of those five hundred fifty years, Celie thought. "I've done much, and seen much, and now I'm tired." He rubbed at his face.

"We brought the Castle here to protect it, and the last of the griffins," Arkwright continued. He was staring at the bricks of the archway as though they had the story inscribed on them. "My people were dying. The Hathelockes, our most bitter enemies, had attacked and killed so many of us. And then the final blow: a sickness swept through the Castle, which brought down both griffin and rider. Those who were not infected were locked into the portions of the Castle that could be spared, and sent here. It was the only thing our wizards could think to do to save us."

"And then what happened?" Celie asked softly.

She was the only one who spoke, or moved. Even Rufus was still, watching Arkwright with his head tilted, his long tail gently sweeping the stones.

"The unicorns," Arkwright said, his face growing even bleaker. "There were unicorns here, in a vast meadow. Carefree, untouched by man or hungry beast. Our griffins had been cooped up too long. Our supplies were low. The moment the stones settled, they leaped from every window and attacked. We could not control them. All we could do was chase the remaining unicorns away. One of our wizards followed, driving them to the sea and making sure that they found safety."

"In Larien," Lilah said slowly. "The stories were true."

Celie wondered if Lilah still wanted a pet unicorn, like she had when she was younger. For a moment she imagined that they could find unicorns in Larien, and bring them back to Sleyne. Lilah would surely be delighted.

Arkwright nodded his head, which was hanging so low that he almost banged his chin on his breastbone, and his shoulders were slumped with regret. "And after all that, the griffins began to sicken and die anyway, and so did many of the riders. We had brought the plague with us, to our great grief. Those of us who survived made a decision. The griffins were gone, our people were almost all gone, and we had only one treasure left to protect: the Castle. The people outside the valley were angry that the unicorns had been killed or exiled. They were afraid of us, with our strange magic and strange ways. We were frightened that they would try to destroy the Castle, or send it—and us—back to our world, where only death awaited us.

"So we did what we could to erase all memory of the Glorious Arkower, our true home. We erased the griffins. We erased the unicorns. We kept our secrets close, destroying or sending back anything that bore images of the griffins or our homeland, any songs or poems that made mention of them. But the Castle . . ." A faint flicker of a smile lit his face. "The Castle cannot be thwarted. The flags could not be changed. Tapestries would appear, we would take them down, and others would replace them.

"My younger brother became the king here. He married a lady of Sleyne, to help appease the people of this land. They called him Glower the First. And when his bride had gone beyond, and he should have been an old man but was not, he turned the throne over to his son and left. I do not know where he went. And even more of our past turned into legend and then faded away, as generations came and went."

"That is terribly sad," Lilah said. Her voice wasn't sad at all, though. She sounded annoyed. "But that doesn't really answer our most urgent questions: How did Celie get an egg to hatch, after all these years? And why is the Castle doing what it's doing right now?"

"Ah, good point, Lilah!" King Glower shook himself.

Like the rest of them, he had been so caught up in Arkwright's story that he'd forgotten why they were here. Even Celie was blinking, clearing her head of the images of dying griffins and frightened unicorns running through the woods.

"I can only guess what has happened back in my world since the days of the plague," Arkwright said. "But something has happened in the last few months that has threatened the Castle and caused it to bring the rest of itself here. There were a few of our people left behind—mostly the dying, but some who refused to leave. I had not thought that there were any griffins left, but perhaps there was one, or perhaps the Castle worked some magic to save that egg until now."

"For Celie," Queen Celina said, and put her arm around Celie's shoulders.

"Yes," Arkwright agreed. He turned and bowed slightly to Celie. "I am sorry, Your Highness, that I accused you of stealing the egg. I can see that you have bonded with this griffin, which indicates that you cared for him tenderly and with a pure heart at his hatching. Otherwise he would not have accepted you."

Celie felt like she herself was flying when he said this. She had been worried for so long that she wasn't taking proper care of Rufus, that she wasn't supposed to have him. And now a wizard, and one who knew griffins, was complimenting her on her griffin training!

"As for the Castle closing a part of itself this way," Arkwright said, indicating the brick wall in front of them, "I can only guess again that it's hiding the things you've collected. Every book that mentions a griffin, every tapestry that depicts one, even the anvil with the old crest of my people has been placed here, in the Castle's Heart. Now it's keeping them safe."

"Safe from whom?" King Glower said.

"Safe from me, I suppose," Arkwright said. "After all, I'm the one who has taken away other books and burned them. I'm the one who smashed the statues that once rested atop the towers, and I have shredded I don't know how many tapestries, and the Castle knows it." He looked ill at the memory. "I thought I was doing it for the good of the Castle," he said, looking pleadingly at King Glower. "I thought I was protecting the last fragments of our people."

"I want to get in there and see what is left," King Glower said decisively. "Also, I need time to think about what's going on. Not the least of which is that my youngest child has been raising a griffin!"

"I've been trying to appeal to the Castle, but it won't

open for me, either," Bran said. He looked wan, and his hands were shaking from pushing so hard against the brick wall. "Perhaps you should try, Father. You are the king, after all."

Looking self-conscious, King Glower went forward and put his hands on the wall. He whispered to the Castle for a moment, while the others all looked elsewhere and tried to give him some privacy. But after a minute or two, he sighed and shook his head.

"I don't think it will listen to me," he said.

"Oh, then the Celie must try," Lulath said. "For it will of a surely let her and the wonderful griffin inside!"

Now it was Celie's turn to feel self-conscious. She moved through the knot of her family to the blocked archway, Rufus following her. She, too, put her hands on the brick wall and bowed her head. Under her breath she muttered a prayer for the Castle to open the archway and let them in.

Nothing happened.

Then Rufus let out a scream and gouged at the bricks with one talon. The bricks melted away, revealing the holiday feasting hall and its strange assortment of tapestries, cloaks, weapons, and memories. Rufus lunged into the room, and the Glower family, Lulath, Pogue, and Wizard Arkwright trailed after him. They all looked around in varying moods of wonder, curiosity, and, in Celie's case, sudden tiredness at the things she and Rolf had collected.

Pogue had also brought some of the things from the

Armor Gallery. There was a sword with a griffin etched on the side of the blade, which was long and curved and heavier at the tip. There was one of the hollow lances that spewed lightning, which had so worried Bran, and which Celie realized she had read about in the book, as well as seen on the cushions—though on the cushions they were just leaning against the rider's shoulder, so no lightning was in evidence.

King Glower looked at the tapestry draped over the table in bemusement. "The clues were all around us," he said. "We just didn't see them." He slumped onto a bench, and the queen sat beside him.

"If the Castle was in danger back in the Glorious Arkower," Queen Celina said, "does that mean we're in any danger? Could something have followed the rest of the Castle here?"

"An excellent point, my love," King Glower said, straightening.

"I doubt it," Arkwright said. "The Castle is all here, and we would know by now if any hostile forces had hidden inside it."

Rufus went over to the leather cloaks and sniffed at them. Then he started chewing on the edge of one, and Celie tried to pull it away. He fought her, so she got Flat Squirrel out of her sash and waved it in his face until he stopped.

"So, will you be able to put back the bits of the Castle we're not using?" King Glower frowned, looking around the room. "This is all very well, I suppose, but I prefer my old throne room. And Ma'am Housekeeper seems to think that all the extra bedrooms and linen closets will just make more work for her staff, not really enhance the Castle."

"I don't really dare, Your Majesty," Arkwright said. "I don't know what's happening on the other end."

"Could we go look?" Rolf asked eagerly. He'd been pacing around the room, but now he came to stand in front of Wizard Arkwright. "Could you and Bran and I, say, go back there and have a look around?"

"Absolutely not," King Glower said. "Much too dangerous!"

"Can such a thing be done?" Bran said. "It's not you bringing the rooms of the Castle here and sending them back when we don't need them. It must be the Castle's own inherent magic. Will the spell that brought it here work both ways?"

"No," Arkwright said. "To protect ourselves, we devised a spell that would only work one way. But you are right: the very stones of which the Castle is built are magic, and it is alive in its own way. Certain parts of it come and go, but to keep it here we rooted many of the rooms, like the main hall and what is now the throne room, to the Sleynth soil; they cannot go back."

"What happens if the Castle isn't under attack anymore?" Lilah said timidly. "What if it decides it's safer to be . . . back where it's from, and leaves? Will we all be left here, or will it take us there?"

"No, no," Arkwright reassured her. "It cannot go all the way back, and it can't take anything vital with it, like a person."

Bran was frowning. He plucked at the pages of the book of Karksus's poetry, and ran a hand over the anvil.

"That's impossible," he said finally. "It goes against every bit of information I've managed to glean about the Castle. It goes against my experience growing up in the Castle, besides. If it can't take anything vital, how did it bring Rufus's egg here? How does it bring the food for the holiday feasts?"

"It's magic—" Arkwright began.

"You and I both know that simply saying something is magic doesn't mean anything," Bran snapped. He folded his arms, rocking back on his heels. "Magic is a science: there are rules. There are rituals and ingredients to any spell. The Castle cannot simply make a feast out of thin air. It could not have saved a living griffin egg for five hundred years and then brought it here, especially if what you say is true. Any transport spell can be reversed—at least, any that I know. And speaking of knowing: knowing the Castle, even if you did root some of the rooms here, it would find a way to move them just to prove that it could!"

Wizard Arkwright closed his eyes. Celie thought he was looking older by the minute. Already thin, he now looked like a stiff breeze might blow him over.

"There was one last step to our spell that assured the Castle would stay in Sleyne," Arkwright said, his voice barely a whisper.

They all moved closer to hear him. Rufus started to snap at the dangling laces of Lulath's sleeve, and Celie brandished Flat Squirrel to make him behave.

"We removed something, something very important to the Castle," Arkwright said. "A part was kept by one who stayed behind in the Glorious Arkower, and a part was kept by me."

"What part?" Bran demanded.

Arkwright pointed to the fireplace. They all looked at the circular indentation on the mantel that had always caught Celie's eye.

"The Eye of the Castle," Arkwright said. "We broke it in half, crippling the Castle, in a sense. My uncle kept half and stayed behind. I took the other half with me."

"Bring it here," Bran said, his voice cold.

"That would be most unwise," Arkwright began.

"I don't care," Bran said. "We live here. This is our Castle now. It chose our family and our father, descended from Hathelockes or not. It chose my little sister to raise what is likely the last griffin in this or any world. Now you tell me that among all your lies and deceptions, you have taken a key part of the Castle and kept it in order to cripple it?" Bran's voice had risen to a shout, and everyone was staring at him in shock. "Bring it here. Now."

Chapter 25

The Eye of the Castle was an enormous round medallion, almost the size of a dinner plate, with a smooth green stone in the center. Around the stone was heavy gold in a pattern of running griffins, and this was what had been broken. Half of it was gone, and Arkwright reluctantly showed them how a post sticking out of the back of the Eye would go into the hole in the mantel and hold it in place.

"My uncle has the missing part," he said.

As he held the broken Eye up to the place where it was supposed to be, Celie felt the Castle ripple under her feet. The rest of her family and Arkwright had felt it, too. Bran's jaw tightened.

"A very grave mistake has been made," King Glower said. His face was pale and his mouth set in a thin line. "A mistake on which my throne rests."

"You aren't to blame, Father," Bran said, his voice hard. "And mistakes can be fixed."

"Even after five hundred years?" King Glower's face went even paler.

"Do they speak of what I think?" Lulath asked the queen.

"They do," she replied. "You're not taking Rolf with you," Queen Celina said to Bran suddenly.

"What?" Rolf looked from their mother to Bran, confused.

Queen Celina ignored her younger son for the moment. "You're going to try to reach the Glorious Arkower, aren't you? Well, fine, you're the Royal Wizard, and I won't try to stop you. But you're not taking Rolf; you're taking armed guards instead."

"We can't," Arkwright bleated.

"Yes, you can," King Glower said in a tone of finality. He stood up and faced Arkwright. "You have wounded the Castle, taken something vital from it. I understand that you thought you were doing the right thing. But still: it's time to restore it. You will take Bran and a handful of soldiers back to the Glorious Arkower, you will make certain that any piece of the Castle left there is not in danger, and you will bring back the other half of the Eye.

"Rolf," the king said, turning to his younger son, "go inform Sergeant Avery that we need him and three of his best men for a short excursion."

Rolf looked like he wanted to argue, probably to try to convince their father that he should be allowed to go, too, but something in King Glower's face stopped him. He jogged out of the room, and they all turned to the king to see what he would say next.

But it was Arkwright who spoke instead.

"This is foolish. There will be nothing there," he said. "My uncle was nearly eight hundred years old when I left; he has probably passed beyond by now. I have no idea who might have the other portion of the Eye."

"We'll just have to look harder, then," Bran said.

"Bran," Celie said. She had to say it again, louder, to get him to pay attention to her. "Bran!" When he looked at her, she said, "Bring back any other griffin eggs you find."

"Ah!" Lulath clapped his hands. "For the Rolf and the Lilah?"

"Absolutely not," Arkwright said. He made a cutting gesture with one hand in the air. "The very idea is appalling! Only the elite of our people were permitted to bond with a griffin. The Castle chose you, and the griffin bonded to you because you undoubtedly have royal Arkower blood on your father's side. Which I can only pray will counteract the Hathelocke blood you've inherited on your mother's side! But if you bring over more eggs, you risk having highly unsuitable people bond with them, and that would lead to . . . to . . ."

"It would lead to nothing but some griffins finding

happy homes with good people," Lilah said with disgust. "You're just a snob."

"What other things do we need for the spell?" Bran demanded.

He took out a small notebook and charcoal pencil and began to make notes. Celie shifted Rufus, who was standing on her foot, aside so that she could take a step forward. Was she really about to witness some real, complicated magic? A gateway to another world sounded far more exotic and dangerous than the workmanlike spells she had seen Bran perform around the castle in the past.

Arkwright began to rattle off a list of herbs and tools. Pogue hurried to clear a space on the largest of the tables, and Lilah and Lulath helped him move the cloaks and books.

Celie found a biscuit in her pocket to keep Rufus busy and sidled closer to Bran. But she didn't take her eyes off Arkwright. He had given in too easily, after so many years of hiding.

"He's up to something," Pogue murmured as he passed near her.

"Undoubtedly," she said softly.

"We will need to use the Eye as a focus," Arkwright said.

He carried it over to the fireplace again.

Celie and Pogue both turned to watch him. Celie tried to get Bran's attention, quietly, but Bran was busy tossing the griffin cushions onto the floor. It occurred to Celie that if this room was the Heart of the Castle, then the fireplace was actually its center. She'd noticed the chimney on her earlier flight: it was round and very tall and crowned with a sort of iron cage to keep birds from flying down it.

Arkwright didn't try to put the Eye back in its place, since there was nothing to hold it there. Instead he laid it on the hearth and ran his hands over it in a loving caress.

The Castle rippled again.

"Even *I* felt that," Pogue said.

"What was that?" Queen Celina said, turning away from the griffin to look first at Bran, then Arkwright. "That keeps happening. It's not quite the headache from the Castle changing around, but what is it?"

"Is that what that funny feeling is?" Lilah shook her head as though trying to cast off the sensation. "That's the Castle changing? I'd never felt it before about a month ago."

"It's because the Castle is more alive now," Arkwright admitted. "I tried to warn you. By putting these things here, in the Heart of the Castle, you've reminded it of what it used to be. Woken it up a little from the necessary sleep we put it in. You're feeling the magic of the Castle more strongly because it's becoming stronger." He looked rather sour at the thought.

Celie was enraged, though. They'd put the Castle to sleep—permanently? They'd taken away a part of it, made it forget what it was? That was something Khelsh would have done! She opened her mouth to say something scathing to Arkwright, but her mother beat her to it.

"You've done a terrible thing," Queen Celina said in her rich voice.

"Mother," Bran began, making a calming gesture. "As a wizard—"

"As the daughter of a wizard, the mother of a wizard, and someone who could have been a wizard herself, I think I do know a bit about magic, Bran," the queen said crisply. Celie gave a little start at that: her mother could have been a wizard? "And I am very angry right now. You've done a terrible thing, and now we will have to make it right," she said to Arkwright, who wouldn't meet her eyes. "You will return to your homeland and bring back the other half of the Eye, to restore the Castle to what it should be. That will be your first step toward making amends for the years of darkness into which you cast the Castle."

"I have to get some things," Arkwright mumbled. He shuffled out of the room, looking like a little boy who had just been scolded. As he passed through the archway, the Castle rippled again.

"Now what?" Lilah sounded almost cross. "I wish the Castle could think of a way to tell us what it wants more specifically."

"It's the Eye," Pogue said. "Bran, I think he took the Eye with him."

"No, it's right there," Bran said, pointing at the hearth without really looking.

"Celie," Lulath said in Grathian. "Really, this griffin is magnificent. I will have my own tailor make you a griffin-riding outfit as a name-day gift!" Rufus, who didn't seem to like most men, was actually letting Lulath stroke his head and had his long tail lovingly coiled around one of Lulath's legs. Celie supposed it was the smell of dog on Lulath that made him seem friendlier than King Glower.

"Thank you," Celie said.

Normally this would have thrilled her, and she definitely needed to find a better solution than hiking up her skirts around her knees. But she couldn't stop staring at the Eye. It didn't look right, somehow. Could Arkwright possibly have switched it? Or made a copy? She remembered some illusions that Bran had made during the winter holidays. The birds and stars that had swirled around this very room had also looked real.

Rolf came back with four soldiers, one of them Sergeant Avery, who had so tirelessly searched for their parents and Bran the year before. The king swiftly told Avery what was happening. To the credit of the sergeant and his men, though their faces paled, they all nodded and stood to the side, ready to go when the wizards told them it was time.

"I'm going to go see if Arkwright needs help," Pogue announced.

"Do you think he ran for it?" Lilah asked in a low voice.

Pogue and Celie looked at her in surprise. She made a face.

"I'm not stupid, you know," she said. "He's a weasel, even if he isn't evil. Which I kind of thought he was, for a while."

She was tugging on one of Rufus's wings, making him stretch it out and then snap it back, which was one of his favorite games to play with Celie. Celie wondered whether Lilah would like a griffin of her own, and decided that she would make an excellent griffin rider. After all, she loved animals, and she could be incredibly persistent.

Pogue just gave a curt nod and headed out of the archway. A moment later he was back, trailing behind Arkwright, who had his arms full of magical supplies. Pogue's face still looked suspicious, but Arkwright didn't seem to notice.

"Are you ready to begin?" Bran asked. He surveyed the room. "Once we mix the herbs and cleanse the bowl to open the gate to your world, will we need anything else?"

"What about ordinary supplies?" Queen Celina asked. "We should pack you some food."

"We'll come back within a day," Bran said. "I just want to see what the situation is there. It's probably too dangerous to stay. And if it isn't, then there's no reason we can't come and go several times."

Arkwright only nodded, a jerky movement. His gaze flicked to the Eye and back. He and Bran began to set out herbs and amulets and all manner of strange, wizardly things. The soldiers stood in a line, and Sergeant Avery talked with the king and queen about how long they planned to be gone and what they might encounter.

"Pogue," Celie whispered. "Keep an eye on Rufus." She was certain that Arkwright had hidden the real Eye, and she wanted to find it before it was too late.

"Right," Pogue whispered back. "Be careful!"

When no one was looking at her, Celie slipped out of the holiday feasting hall. It would be odd calling it the Heart of the Castle, but she supposed she would have to get used to it.

The Castle was nearly twice the size of what she was used to, and Arkwright could have hidden the Eye anywhere. It was most likely in his rooms, though, so she went that way. He hadn't been gone long, after all, and he'd brought back the herbs and tools he needed. He probably hadn't thought that they would guess what he'd done, and had just stuffed the Eye in a wardrobe or something.

She passed several members of the court in the corridor. They looked at her curiously, and she nodded and walked even more quickly past them. They wanted to know what was going on, with the Castle, with the griffin she'd flown into the courtyard earlier, but there was no time.

Lord Sefton, however, stopped her.

"Princess Cecelia," he said with a bow. "A word?"

There were a few other councilors standing behind him, looking equally curious. She supposed that he was their chosen delegate, since he was known to be a favorite of the Glower family.

"I'm in a hurry, my lord," she said, continuing to walk. He followed her. "So let me just tell you: Yes, I have a griffin that I hatched from an egg the Castle gave me. Bran and Wizard Arkwright are preparing to travel to the world where the Castle was born, to see if they can . . . well, they're going to try to help the Castle so that it stops doing . . . what it's doing." She was panting slightly from walking rapidly and talking at the same time.

"Is there anything we can do?" Lord Sefton asked.

That was another reason Celie liked him: no criticizing or pointless hand-wringing, despite the startled look on his face at what she'd just said.

"Keep everyone out of the holiday feasting hall," she instructed. "And let them know that all is well, and my father will be giving more details later." She was sure that last was true. It was what her father did, after all.

"Very good." Sefton took his fellow councilors and headed down a cross-corridor toward the councilors' privy chamber.

Celie had reached Arkwright's rooms, and took a deep breath before trying the door. It was locked. She wiggled the latch, and felt just the faintest twinge in her head. The door swung open.

The room was very tidy. Celie could see exactly where he had grabbed up some tools from the array on the table, and bundles of herbs from the well-organized shelves. The bed was neatly made, the wardrobe door closed and latched. Celie ran over and opened it, releasing a scent of lavender and revealing a row of plain gray robes. She pulled them off their hooks, not caring about the mess, and flung them on the floor. Nothing.

She turned and threw herself flat on the floor, groping under the bed. Nothing. She checked under the pillows, and in the little cabinet by the side of the bed. Nothing there, either. She checked the chamber pot, since this room didn't have a water closet, but it was empty (and blessedly clean).

She turned around again, searching the room. And that was when she noticed a narrow door. It was half-hidden behind the window curtains, and Celie couldn't remember seeing it before. Of course, she couldn't remember whether she'd been in this room before, either. It was one of the guest rooms, one that only used to appear when very important guests arrived.

Celie went through the door and found a narrow corridor—one of the secret passageways that ran through the Castle!

The passageway was dark, but there was a smell of lamp oil in the air. Celie's heart pounded: she was sure that Arkwright had come this way. She heard a noise and turned quickly, frightened that Arkwright had followed her, but there was no one there. She steeled herself and continued on.

She passed one door, but the latch felt gritty with dust, so she kept going. The passageway ended in a door with a clean latch, and she pushed it open and shoved aside the tapestry that covered the opening. The threshold was higher than she'd expected, and she fell into the room.

And bounced.

Chapter 26

It was the room with the bouncy floor. The floor was some sort of slick, black material, held taut at the walls with steel fittings, which allowed you to jump much higher than you normally could. Celie looked around. The main door to the room was across from her, and she bounced her way over to it, but it was locked from the other side. Celie looked around, and then up, bouncing herself gently while she thought.

About ten feet up was a small ledge. She could barely see a hint of something gold sitting on it.

"There you are," she said aloud.

She jumped. And jumped again. She and Rolf had spent many afternoons in the bouncy-floored room, and she knew that it would take a while to build up some height. It would have helped if Rolf were there to give her a lift; they'd developed a way of launching each other that let them go much higher. Celie jumped again, but still fell several feet short of reaching the ledge.

She bounced over to the one window, which was a few paces away from the ledge, and slightly lower. She bounced up and tried to land on the windowsill, but it was too narrow. She jumped, caught the latch, and swung the window open. On her next jump she landed on the windowsill and barely caught herself before she pitched right out and into the moat.

She grabbed the edge of the window tightly. Then she closed her eyes and held on as the Castle rippled. And rippled again. There was a groan, and a sound like sliding stones.

"Oh, no," Celie said. "What's happening now?"

She looked out the window but couldn't see anything. She wished Rufus were there: it would be easy to fly him up to the ledge. She thought about whistling for him, but didn't think even his keen ears would hear. Still, she sent out a sort of silent call.

Rufus, come to me.

The Castle rippled again, and she clung to the copper window frame.

When that ripple passed, she took her chance. She threw herself down as hard as she could, feeling the floor dip beneath her feet almost to the height of her knees. Then the floor snapped her back up, and she stretched out her fingers for the ledge. She just barely caught her fingers on the Eye, and then her cheek and shoulder slammed into the stones of the wall. She fell back onto the floor, which bounced her six more times before she came to rest. A little dizzy, shoulder and face throbbing, she looked around.

She'd knocked the Eye off the ledge, and it was sitting on the floor by her feet. With a crow of triumph she picked it up and tucked it into her bodice. The Castle rippled again, and groaned, and she headed for the secret door.

Rawk, came Rufus's cry from the open window.

Celie whirled, and there he was, staring in at her with his wings pumping to keep him level. She bounced back up to the window and climbed out and onto his back.

"That's my wonderful boy," she said, stroking his neck. "My clever boy! Take us to the courtyard!"

Rufus wheeled around and flew up and over the Castle walls. From her vantage point in the air, Celie watched the stones of the courtyard ripple. She could see that the stables were abuzz with activity as the grooms tried to calm the horses, and saw two guards head for the gatehouse at a dead run.

Rufus had barely come to rest on the ground when Rolf ran out to meet them, his face white.

"Something's wrong," he shouted before Celie could dismount. "The hall closed up as soon as they started the spell, and everyone else is inside! Have you got the real Eye?"

"Yes!"

The Castle groaned.

"Bring it! We'll have to try to break in! Or—"

"No!" Celie had an exploding feeling in her chest, a dryness in her throat that told her she needed to get the Eye to the Heart of the Castle with all possible speed. She knew it, she knew it, she felt it beating inside her. She gripped the handles of the harness.

There had to be a faster, better way. Rufus pawed at the courtyard paving and Celie shifted on his back, her skirt catching the harness. She really needed to get a riding dress made like . . . The leather cloaks! "Rufus, take us up!" Rufus sprang into the air, and Celie called down to Rolf, "I'm going to throw it down the chimney!"

She didn't know whether the Castle was in distress because Arkwright was doing something deliberately to ruin the spell, or if the spell was simply going wrong because they weren't using the real Eye.

She guided Rufus over the rooftops to the curved roof of the Heart. There was the chimney, jutting upward with its iron cage on top. When Rufus was hovering over the chimney, she looked down. It wasn't big enough for Rufus to perch on, and there was no way she could pry the bars aside. She would have to drop the Eye down as carefully as she could, to make sure it didn't just bounce off the bars or shatter.

She held tightly to Rufus's sides with her knees. Leaning as far over his shoulder as she dared, she pulled out the

Eye. She tried to hold it over a space between two bars, despite Rufus bobbing up and down in the air. With a little prayer and then a scream, she let the Eye fall.

It passed between the bars and fell out of sight. Celie counted to five, and when nothing happened she brought Rufus around and they headed toward the courtyard again.

Only then was there an explosion that seemed to lift up each stone of the Castle and set it down again. Rufus stumbled as he landed, the stones of the courtyard rising up and back again under his talons. Rolf fell down the steps and hit his chin, coming up with blood running down the front of his tunic and his eyes wild.

"Are you all right?" he and Celie called to each other at the same time.

"I'm fine," Celie said.

She dismounted and led Rufus up the steps, meeting Rolf and hurrying inside the Castle with him. The explosion had thrown the doors open, and the guards had fallen down as well. They were just getting up, shaking their heads and checking for their weapons, when Celie and Rolf swept by.

"Thank heavens," Rolf said, speeding up. "It's open again!"

They skidded into the Heart of the Castle, as Celie now found herself calling it in her mind. Rufus didn't stop fast enough and nearly knocked Celie down, but Lulath reached out and caught her. The Castle rippled again, and she found herself clutching at Rufus with one hand and Lulath with the other to stay upright.

"What have you done?" Bran roared at Arkwright.

"It should have worked," Arkwright babbled. "Why didn't it work?" He scrabbled in the remains of the spell on the table.

Everything had been thrown around by the explosion. Lilah leaned on Lulath with one hand to her cheek as if something had struck her, and King Glower was sitting on a bench looking dazed while Queen Celina hovered over him. The tapestry was on the floor in a heap, and so were the lances and cloaks. The guards had their weapons out but didn't seem to know where to point them or what to do.

"Celie threw the Eye down the chimney," Rolf blurted out.

The Castle rumbled, and Lulath reached out his free hand and caught Lilah before she could fall.

"You did what?" Arkwright's face twisted with rage. "No, no! Don't you see? We can't go back! We can never go back!"

They all froze, his words hanging in the air.

"Then where were you taking Bran?" Queen Celina demanded.

Everyone circled around Arkwright. Sergeant Avery had one hand on the hilt of his sword, and both Pogue's hands were fists. Arkwright looked like he was going to protest his innocence, but then he sagged.

"To another world; an empty one," he admitted. He hurried to the fireplace. "The Eye must be taken far from here, now. The Castle must go back to sleep! The old world will bring only death!"

"You're insane," Bran said. "Can't you hear that? We need the Eye to try to find a way to soothe the Castle. It's fighting with every stone to undo what you've done. I think it's clear that it won't let us take anything away from it ever again."

The rumbling was getting louder. The flagstones were vibrating beneath their feet, making Celie's toes feel numb. She was having trouble thinking clearly as Arkwright's story and his repeated attempts to trick them swirled around in her head. To add to it all, her shoulder and cheek were throbbing with pain where she had bruised them while retrieving the Eye.

There was shouting from the main hall, and Rufus raised his head and screamed a challenge. He buffeted Celie with his wings, trying to shoo her to safety in a corner of the room, his tail lashing.

"Let's take him out into the main hall," Rolf called to Celie. He had to raise his voice to be heard. "Less crowded there."

"But if Bran needs help—" Celie began.

Rufus came up close behind her and dipped and rolled his shoulder. Celie found herself knocked over his right wing and lying upside down on his back. Rolf put one hand on Celie's shoulder to steady her and the other on Rufus's back, and started to lead him out the door.

"Are you all right?" Pogue ran into the Heart as they were headed out. There was sweat darkening his hair and the neck of his tunic. "I went out to look for you when the archway opened, Celie. There's black smoke coming out of all the chimneys, and the outer wall has started crumbling again."

"Everyone get out," King Glower ordered. "Rolf! Pogue! Take Celie!" He grabbed Bran's arm. "Tell me what I can do!"

Lilah and Lulath started for the door as well, and Celie saw Bran pick up a long silver rod, a grim look on his face. Then Pogue and Rolf hustled Rufus out into the main hall with Celie hanging the wrong way across his back. They let her sit up once they were out of shouting range of the Heart of the Castle. She tried not to rub her shoulder: they were already treating her like a baby or an invalid; they didn't need to know she was really hurt. Besides which, it wasn't all that bad.

Rolf led them into the corridor where Celie's bedroom was, but then there was a twist and it all changed. Rolf held up a hand in warning.

"Where are we?" Pogue asked. He tugged at the harness to make Rufus stop. The rumbling was so loud he had to shout to be heard even at close range. "I've never seen this corridor before."

"Where's your atlas, Cel?" Rolf asked, his voice strained.

"It's useless now," Celie told him. "This corridor isn't on there. I've never seen it before, either." She looked around, nervously stroking Rufus's neck.

There was no sign of the main hall behind them. The corridor seemed to go on and on in both directions, although it was hard to tell. The lamps weren't lit and there were no windows; there could be a staircase or a sudden drop into the dungeon waiting just a few paces ahead, and they wouldn't know until they fell. Lilah and Lulath had left the Heart just a few steps behind them, but there was no sign of them now.

"I have no idea where we are," Celie admitted.

"That's not possible," Rolf said, sounding desperate.

They went forward for a few paces, but there was still nothing. No doors, no windows, no lamps, no stairs. Pogue called out, but there was no answer. They turned back, and found that the corridor ended right behind them.

But when they turned around again, there was a single lamp, its flame quivering as the Castle shook, and a spiral staircase that led upward. It would be barely big enough for Rufus. They looked at each other and shrugged. Celie got off Rufus's back, and they started to climb.

They didn't climb long. The spiral stair brought them to a round tower that Celie had never seen before. Judging from Rolf's and Pogue's expressions, they'd never seen it before, either. It looked most like the hatching tower, with a sloping floor and four large open windows, but there was no nest or any sign of an egg. The view out the windows showed Celie that it stood between the hatching tower and the north tower, and she could see another tower far across the Castle from them that looked new as well.

Rufus immediately went to a window and began screeching, trying to get Celie to fly with him.

"No, Rufus! Not now," Celie said. She reached for his harness to pull him away.

There was a great crash, and a shudder. Rufus was thrown back from the window and Celie fell to the floor beside him, banging her knees painfully on the stone floor. Pogue hit his head on the edge of a window and crashed to the floor, moaning. Rolf dropped to all fours and crawled to Pogue as the Castle settled itself.

There was an enormous heave, as though the Castle were trying to break free from the ground. Celie closed her eyes and clung to Rufus. Her hair stood on end, and the twisting sensation at the back of her head was so strong that it nearly made her vomit. When it stopped, she was too weak to raise her head for a few heartbeats.

The silence made Celie's ears ring. She finally opened her eyes and looked around, but was still too weak to get up.

"All right, Cel?" Rolf said. He was sprawled on the floor beside Pogue, and had to cough first in order to get the words out.

"Fine," Celie rasped, her voice just as raw. She pointed at Pogue. "What about him?"

Rolf checked Pogue and then nodded. "He's all right, I think." He slapped Pogue's face gently. "Wake up, Pogue!"

Rufus wanted to stand up, so Celie used him to get unsteadily to her feet as well. He leaned against her, and she spent a moment soothing him. Pogue groaned, and Rolf helped him sit up. Celie gave them both a tremulous smile.

"There we go," Rolf said approvingly.

Pogue took a few deep breaths and touched the growing lump on his temple. "Ow," he said.

"You'll be fine," Rolf assured him.

Celie coughed again and smoothed the feathers on Rufus's head. Then she looked out the window.

"Is it bleeding?" Pogue asked Rolf.

"You'll be fine," Rolf said again, not really answering the question. "But it looks like our staircase is gone, so I'll sit here with you while Celie flies down for help. All right, Cel?"

Celie didn't answer.

"Cel! Are you hurt?" Rolf started to scramble to his feet.

"She's white as milk," Pogue said. "Where are you hurt?"

"I'm not hurt," Celie whispered.

"Cel," Rolf said in concern as he steadied himself on a windowsill. "You look like— By my aunt's hairy toes!"

"What is it?" Pogue demanded.

He tried to get up and slumped down again, dizzy, but Rolf and Celie didn't help him. Neither of them could move. They were frozen, staring out the window.

"The Castle's gone," Celie said, her voice shaking.

They were in a tower—a single tower in the middle of a forest, surrounded by jagged mountains. Here and there through the trees they could see piles of stones that might have been ruins of other towers, or walls, or even whole rooms. A little distance away was another tower, identical to theirs. It might have been the same one where Rufus hatched, but Celie couldn't be sure.

"What is it?" Pogue asked again.

Celie spared him a glance. His face was white, bordering on green, and there was a small thread of blood oozing from his head wound. He was swaying from side to side, and she didn't think he would be able to stand.

Unable to stop herself, Celie looked out the window again. Nothing out there was familiar. Nothing.

"I think . . . I think we're in the Glorious Arkower," Rolf said, and his voice sounded very young.

"Impossible," Pogue said. He sounded like he might be sick.

"The Glorious Arkower," Rolf repeated. "The Castle's own world."

"Are you sure?" Pogue asked. "Celie? Do you think so, too?"

Celie looked down at him again, her heart thudding irregularly in her chest. Pogue's voice was weak, and his eyes looked glassy. He started to slump forward, and Rolf dived down and caught him as he fainted again.

Celie moved to help, but something outside caught her eye. She moved to the nearest window instead and peered out. Rufus crowded against her side and she pushed him back, not wanting him to take off into this strange world.

"What is it?" Rolf had eased Pogue to the floor and was chafing his wrists to try to restore his blood flow.

"Oh, no," Celie said. "Oh, no! No!"

"What is it?" Rolf left Pogue and joined her at the window.

"It's Lilah and Lulath," Celie said, and a sob tore its way through her chest.

"No! They're trapped here, too? Where?"

Unable to speak, Celie pointed to the other tower. She could see a figure all in bright yellow there, waving its arms. It was Lulath. Behind him was a flicker of blue: Lilah. Rolf waved his arms in response and then turned to Celie.

"We're all trapped here," she said. She pointed to where the stairs had been. There was nothing: no stairs, not even a door. "We're all trapped."

"Celie," Rolf said, taking her by the shoulders. "It will be all right. I want you to fly Rufus over to Lilah and Lulath, and see if you can't bring them back here. We need to make a plan."

"A plan for what?" She realized that she was gripping a handful of Rufus's feathers and quickly released him. "Rolf, we're stuck in the Glorious Arkower, a place so dangerous that a five-hundred-year-old wizard didn't want to come back to it! I don't know what you're planning for, but I'm planning on sitting here and waiting for Bran to rescue us!" She took a deep breath, trying to steady herself.

"Oh, really?" Rolf said. "We're in another world, Cel! A world that contains flocks of griffins! Or . . . it used to, anyway! Are you really going to just sit here in a tower and wait to be rescued?"

Celie felt a bubbling in her stomach at Rolf's words. They were in a different world. And there might be other griffins left. She remembered her daydream before Rufus hatched, where she delivered a healthy young roc back to its noble parents. If they really were in the Glorious Arkower, then it was possible that Rufus's parents were somewhere nearby.

She glanced at Pogue. He was starting to perk up, and his injury didn't look all that bad. Her bruised arm was feeling better already. And Bran would probably come to get them soon. It would be a shame not to do just a little exploring.

"Let me see if I can get Lilah and Lulath," Celie said, making up her mind. She swung onto Rufus's back. "And we'll make a plan."

"For getting home?" Rolf raised his eyebrows.

"First things first," Celie told him. "We need to figure out where the rest of the griffins have gone."

Celie and Rufus leaped out of the window and started soaring toward the other tower. But Celie looked back at Rolf and Pogue and called out, "Then we'll find our way home."

Acknowledgments

As much as I enjoyed writing about the further adventures of Celie and Castle Glower, this book really took the mickey out of me! It was the most complicated journey that any of my books has ever taken, and I would like to thank, from the depths of my heart, everyone who helped Celie and Castle Glower and all their friends (old and new).

First off, my dear, long-suffering husband. Poor man. Puts in a full day of work at his office, then has to come home, cook, clean, and tuck the kids into bed . . . and he never complains! Never! (Well, maybe there was one time . . . but still!) And my poor kids, who are so good about playing quietly while I work and rant and pace and steal their Easter/Halloween/Christmas candy! Thank you, all of you!

Thank you to my extended family: parents, siblings,

and in-laws. Aunts and uncles and cousins who share my books with friends and students, you are wonderful! And a special shout-out to my dear aunt Shirley, who called me the day of my thrice-extended-deadline, out of the blue, to tell me that she'd just finished *Tuesdays at the Castle* and loved it so much she just couldn't wait for the sequel. I needed that, Shirley. Thank you.

Speaking of thrice-extended-deadlines: thank you, Michelle Nagler, Editor from Heaven! Thank you, thank you, thank you for patiently helping me through the many drafts and missed deadlines and hair-pulling hysteria of this book. And for figuring out where the thing with the maps in the room with the guy had gone.

Special thanks to all the Bloomsbury team, for their tireless help and endless enthusiasm: Katy Hershberger, Bridget Hartzler, Brett Wright, Rachel Stark, Beth Eller, Linette Kim, Caroline Abbey—so much fabulousness! And extra-special thanks to copyeditor Linda Minton: bless you for your astute comments and help in the final stages of this book!

Thank you, thank you, a thousand times thank you to Amy-My-Awesome-Agent, for never being less than wonderful, for never losing your cool, for being a good friend, and for being a stellar agent and advisor.

And my little one-dimpled, dark-eyed Baby Roo, the youngest of my three children, has been with me for every moment of this book. I started writing it during my pregnancy, I worked on it during those horrible eleven days he was in the NICU (big hugs to Adriana and Shad, Bev, Dr. Bentley and Dr. Jason, though), and I finished it with him cuddled up in my lap. Baby Roo, this is your book, my love! (Now stop chewing on it!)

Read on for a glimpse of Celie's adventures at Castle Glower on Thursday . . .

You are not leaving me behind," Celie repeated.

Rolf and Lilah exchanged looks, and Celie could see her brother and sister preparing to side against her. She braced herself.

"Someone needs to stay here with Pogue," Lilah said in a wheedling voice.

"But you could stay with Pogue," Celie retorted. "You don't want to get dirty hiking around the forest, do you?"

She knew that she had Lilah there. Lilah was already upset that they'd had to sleep on the hard stone floor of this run-down hatching tower last night. They didn't have any water for drinking, let alone washing, and Lilah was looking as mussed as anyone had ever seen her.

Lilah ran her fingers through her hair, caught them on a snarl, and straightened. "I . . . I . . . Listen to me, Celie," she said. "We don't know what's out there. We don't know if we're alone, or if there are people right outside this tower, and if those people are dangerous. We don't know what animals are out there."

"You think that I don't know that?" Celie looked at her sister in disbelief. Did Lilah think she was an infant? Not only that, this was the third time at least that they'd had this argument.

Here they were, in the Glorious Arkower, the land where her beloved Castle had been built, and they wanted her to sit. And wait. And listen to Pogue snore. Her feet positively itched with the need to get out of this cramped tower and explore—but no, it was not allowed!

Celie paced around the edges of the tower, which didn't take long, while Rolf and Lilah watched her. They were both working up more reasons for her to stay behind while they explored; she could see the wheels turning in both their brains.

It was true that someone needed to watch their friend Pogue. He had hit his head during the confusion that had brought them from Sleyne, which fortunately had been the only injury. They'd thought the Castle was trying to shake itself to pieces, or that there was a mighty storm caught in its walls, and then suddenly the tower that Celie, Pogue, Rolf, and her griffin Rufus were taking shelter in had been ripped free and brought here.

Celie and Rolf had looked out of the wide arched windows, across an expanse of trees, and seen another tower, with Lilah and Prince Lulath waving at them frantically from the windows. Celie had flown Rufus across to collect them, and they'd all spent a long, cold night on the floor, with an icy wind blowing through the open window arches, carrying strange noises and scents with it. In the morning, Rolf had announced that he and Lilah alone would explore the surrounding forest while Celie kept an eye on Pogue, and Lulath looked for water.

"Now Celie," Rolf began, "you are the youngest, so it makes more sense." He seemed pleased with this logic, but Celie was not.

Celie honestly couldn't believe that they were doing this to her. Celie was the one the Castle loved best. She was the one who had raised and trained a griffin. She was the one who had found the broken piece of the Eye and restored it to its rightful place in the Heart of the Castle, what her family had always called the holiday feasting hall. She'd hoped it would help the Castle, which had been acting strangely for months: adding new rooms, refusing to take away unused ones, even bringing a tower with a live griffin egg inside. But once the Eye was in place, the Castle had nearly flown to bits, and brought them to the Glorious Arkower, presumably to find the other piece of the Eye, which Celie had proposed the night before, and which they had all agreed was the right thing to do. And now she was the one being told to stay safe, sit quietly, and make sure that Pogue was still breathing.

He snored again.

He was breathing.

The truth was that Celie was terrified of the Glorious Arkower. She'd never even been outside of Sleyne . . . not to Grath or Vhervhine or any of their neighboring countries, and now here she was in a whole new world! A world where she and her siblings and their friends were strangers, with no clue how to find food or water . . . or a way home. A world where something, some threat, had made the Castle gather up every last room, corridor, and stable left in the Glorious Arkower, and plop them down in Sleyne.

What could threaten a castle? What could threaten *the* Castle?

But when Celie was frightened of something, she liked to face it head-on. She did not like to sit in a cold stone room and worry, but that is exactly what they wanted her to do. And to cap it all off, when Lulath had gone searching for water, Rufus had gone with him. Her own griffin had left her behind.

"I need to go with you," Celie said to Rolf, trying to sound capable, and not whiny. "We need to find the missing piece of the Eye so we can go home and heal the Castle."

"We can look for it," Lilah said immediately.

"What if Lulath and Rufus have gotten into trouble?" Celie countered. "A young griffin, wandering around with . . . Lulath?" She raised her eyebrows.

"There might be griffins everywhere here," Lilah said. "It could be that they've found a village and are getting help." Her face brightened as she hit on this idea. "Yes, that's undoubtedly what's happened."

"And if they were in trouble, I'm sure Rufus would be able to fly straight back here to you," Rolf said. "They're fine."

"Makes sense," Pogue suddenly called out, stopping mid-snore. Then he rolled over and went back to sleep.

Lilah and Celie exchanged worried looks over Pogue's head, but Rolf shrugged.

"Lulath said he'd do that," Rolf reminded them.

Lulath claimed that Pogue suffered from a cracked skull.

"He is needing the sleep, but not too much, and the quiet, of that a lot," Lulath had told them with his thick Grathian accent. "We must be waking him at that quarter of each hour, and watching to see that the breathing is clear. But of a certainty the swaying when standing and the sick of the stomach and hurting of head will soon be gone! And he is probably talking with strange words and perhaps sleeping while talking for a time, too."

That had been a great relief, as Lilah had been certain that Pogue was dying. Celie was relieved, too. She hadn't thought that Pogue was dying, not really, but she had thought that his injuries might be permanent.

Pogue let out another snore and Celie paced the tower again. It was a hatching tower, with just one circular room with a sloping floor and a trapdoor that led down a narrow staircase to a small door at the base of the tower. It had no furnishings and no coverings on the wide windows, but they were fortunate that, unlike the tower where Rufus had hatched, this one had a roof. The worst part about the tower was that it appeared to be dead: there was no friendly hum, no feeling of warmth coming from these stones, for all that this tower had been a part of the Castle in Sleyne barely a day before.

Celie stopped pacing and stared out again, looking for Lulath and Rufus, but all she saw were trees. Strange trees, with very straight, slim trunks, branches so evenly placed that they looked man-made, and dark-green needles instead of leaves. Away to the right there was something that might have been a lake or a plain, and beyond that, three sharply pointed mountains rose against a faintly purple sky. At the foot of the tower was a damaged expanse of stones that had probably been the rear courtyard of the Castle five hundred years ago, and there was a broken-down stable and the other hatching tower. It was all very horrible and bleak.

In the distance was a haze of smoke that looked as though it might be from a largish village or even a town, but Rolf had deemed it too far away to reach. They would have to hack their way through miles of forest to get there, so they had decided that the two of them were going to strike out toward the lake and hope that there was a farm or house hidden in the forest closer to the ruins.

And it seemed that by the two of them, Rolf meant himself and Lilah.

Rolf looked at Celie. His face was stern, and he looked as he had a year ago, when he'd briefly been the king in their father's place. Lilah folded her arms, looking very much like their mother.

Celie sighed and sagged against the window frame.

They both kissed her, then went down the trapdoor and out of the tower, leaving her alone with Pogue.

Celie had longed all her life for a truly grand adventure, but now that she was having one she found it quite lacking. Lacking in food. Lacking in blankets. Lacking in adventure, really.

After what she thought was about a quarter of an hour, but was probably much less, since time seemed to have slowed down, she woke Pogue. He sat up and talked to her for a while and she made him tell her his name and the names of all eight of his siblings, from his sister Jane Marie on down to baby Ava, to make sure his brain was working. Then she let him go back to sleep.

And she went back to waiting by the window.

She had almost dozed off herself, slumped on the broad windowsill, when she saw the other griffins.

Griffins.

Celie felt as though she'd been struck by lightning, and she could only gasp and stare as a griffin broke out of the trees away to the left, circled twice over the ruined courtyard, and then dived into the forest again. Celie screamed with excitement. She leaned out of the window, trying to catch sight of it again, when two smaller griffins burst out of the forest, chased by the first one she'd seen. The smaller griffins fled, screeching, while the larger one turned back and flew toward the ruins of the stable. It landed and went inside, and Celie nearly fell out of the window trying to see if there were more griffins waiting for it.

More griffins?

Her heart was racing. She gripped the stone windowsill until her joints ached, and she let out another scream. She had just seen three griffins! *Three!* She danced in place, stomping her feet on the stone floor. Pogue snored on while Celie jumped and clapped her hands.

The emblem of Castle Glower was a tall tower with three griffins flying over it, but until this last year she (and everyone else in Sleyne) had thought that griffins were merely legends. Then her stuffed toy lion, Rufus, had turned into one and eaten horrible Prince Khelsh of Vhervhine, after he had put the Castle to sleep and tried to kill her family. Rufus the Stuffed-Lion Griffin had disappeared, and she had found Rufus the Real-Life Griffin's egg some eight months later. Having seen two real griffins in her life, Celie considered herself to be fabulously lucky, particularly since both the griffins had, essentially, been for her.

And now she'd seen three more.

And one of the three was only a stone's throw away from her tower, in the half-caved-in stables. Did it live there? Celie wondered how many griffins were left in the Glorious Arkower.

Wizard Arkwright, who had come to the Castle to figure out why it was bringing the new rooms willy-nilly, had admitted that he was the one who had brought the Castle to Sleyne centuries before, because all the griffins and their riders were dying of a plague. Most of the riders who made it to Sleyne had died shortly after arriving, already sick themselves though they hadn't known it, and all their griffins had died.

But it appeared that Arkwright was wrong, or maybe he'd lied. The griffin in the stable was almost as large as a horse, and gleamed golden in the dim sunlight. The other two had been much smaller, and brown, but griffins all the same. Celie just had to get a closer look.

"Pogue!"

She jumped down from the window.

"Pogue, wake up!" Celie shook his shoulder. "Wake up a moment."

"Huh? All right?" Pogue blinked at her.

"I'm fine but I need to leave the tower," Celie said.

"No," Pogue said, more alert. "We're not leaving the tower."

He tried to sit up twice before finally succeeding, and Celie pushed him gently back down before he could stand. He wheezed and leaned his head back against the cold stone wall, his face gray.

"I have to . . ." Celie stopped herself before she said, "see the griffins." Instead she looked away in unfeigned embarrassment and said, "I have to, er, *you know*."

Pogue's pale cheeks flushed.

"All right, all right," he said. "But hurry and don't go far!" Then he blushed even more deeply. "I mean . . . be careful!"

"I will," she promised.

And she would. Just as soon as she had a look around that stable.

Celie almost flew down the spiral stairs to the bottom of the tower. Outside she looked around for Lulath and Rufus, and was both relieved and disappointed when she didn't see them. She supposed it was better that Rufus not run into any hostile griffins, but she knew that Lulath would be up for the adventure of exploring the stable, and he *was* reassuringly tall and strong despite his fancy clothes.

She hurried over the uneven stones of the ruined courtyard, which she thought would probably go at the back of the Castle, near the other griffin stable, if the Castle were whole. It made her head feel funny to try to imagine the Castle all here, put together correctly. That thought raised another question: Did the rooms grow and stretch and disappear when the Castle was in the Glorious Arkower the way they did in Sleyne? She would have to ask Wizard

Arkwright, if they ever went home, and if he could be forced to tell the truth.

When. When they went home.

Celie stopped short of the stable, trying to peer inside without being seen. The sun was high overhead, but there was something smoky about the air here, although it didn't smell like smoke and nothing was on fire that she could see. The sun was dark orange, and the haze in the sky made it impossible to see anything inside the stable. Celie took another step forward.

A furious mass of golden feathers and fur exploded out of the dark doorway.

Celie screamed as she was thrown to the rough stones. The griffin stood over her, one talon piercing the shoulder of her gown, pinning her to the ground. Celie continued to scream and so did the griffin. It opened its beak wide and leaned toward her face. She threw up her free hand to protect her eyes, and felt the smooth beak smack into her palm.

But instead of biting off her hand—which it was large enough to do without blinking—the griffin sniffed her palm. Then it sniffed down her arm, tilting its head forward so that the round nostrils atop the beak could get closer to her skin. It sniffed her clothes, her hair, and her neck and face. It tickled but Celie was too terrified to laugh, so she just lay there and shook.

The griffin finally raised its head just enough to look at

her. Celie gazed back at the round golden eye, trying to appear friendly and not too terrified.

The griffin suddenly screeched, which made Celie shriek in reply, but she got herself under control again after a moment. There was a scraping of talons from the stable and then another griffin joined them. Celie turned her head slightly to look at it. It was smaller than the one holding her down, and moved in a more graceful and less aggressive way that Celie found reassuring. Another screech, neither as loud nor as menacing as the first, and the smaller griffin edged forward and also sniffed Celie from head to toe.

To Celie's shock, the smaller griffin began to coo, and rubbed its head against her cheek. The feathers tickled her nose and Celie sneezed, which startled them all, but the larger griffin didn't attack. Instead, it pulled its talon out of her gown and took a step back. It clacked its tongue at Celie, and when she didn't move it nudged her with a talon until she sat up. Trying not to make any sudden moves, Celie stood and the larger griffin started butting her with its head, guiding her toward the stable, which was dark inside and potentially held other, less friendly griffins. As much as she wanted to see how these griffins lived, she was beginning to regret not dragging Pogue along with her.

But the large griffin would not accept her muttered excuses and attempts to dodge away. It steered her through the doorway and into the stable. The light coming in through the holes in the roof showed Celie that it was identical to the griffin stable that had recently appeared in Sleyne, though in far worse repair. Also, this one was being lived in. The stall doors had been ripped away, and the stalls were filled with nests of bracken and grass. There was a neat pile of bones in one corner, and a pile of nutshells in another.

Celie looked around their stable and then nodded and smiled broadly. "It's very nice," she said in a bright voice, speaking slowly. "Very nice indeed!"

Did they understand Sleynth? Probably not, but hopefully they would interpret her expression and words as friendly.

The smaller griffin fussed around her, batting her softly with upraised wings that had a slight cream-colored pattern on them. Celie tripped over a stick on the floor and fell into the side of one of the stalls. She took a step back to brace herself, and something hard under her foot rolled away. She almost fell right on top of the smaller, gold-and-cream griffin.

"Oof! Sorry!" She caught hold of the side of the stall and pulled herself upright, then looked down to see what she had stepped on.

It wasn't a rock but an irregular chunk of crystal. It was probably clear, and had some green color to it, but it was so dirty that she couldn't really tell. There was a clump of mud and a dingy feather stuck to one side. Celie picked it up, intending to toss it out a window into the forest. Lying on a rock was probably uncomfortable for whatever griffin slept in that stall. It was so dirty that her palms began to itch, and she wondered if Lulath would find enough water for drinking and washing. She didn't want to think about what was coating that rock.

When the gold-and-cream griffin saw what Celie was holding, however, it hissed and raised its wings. Immediately the larger griffin came down the aisle. It had something in its beak and tossed it at Celie's feet before lunging at her, snatching the crystal out of her hands. It backed down the aisle, glaring, and hid the thing in another stall. Belatedly Celie remembered Rufus's fondness for squirreling away jewelry and other shiny objects. He'd made off with her gold circlet shortly before a state dinner just last week, and he'd shrieked at her when she'd retrieved it from under his bed.

She held up her hands, fingers splayed, to show that she didn't have any more of their treasures, then looked down to see what the large griffin had dropped at her feet. It looked like a dead rabbit, and she said a silent prayer that they wouldn't offer her some raw meat and become offended when she didn't eat it.

"Oh," she said, looking down at the thing. "Rufus."

Then her knees buckled and she sat down in the bracken of the nest.

It was her old stuffed toy lion. Here at her feet. In the Glorious Arkower.

JESSICA DAY GEORGE

is the *New York Times* bestselling author of the Tuesdays at the Castle series, the Dragon Slippers series, and the Twelve Dancing Princesses series, as well as *Silver in the Blood* and *Sun and Moon, Ice and Snow*. Originally from Idaho, she studied at Brigham Young University and worked as a librarian and bookseller before turning to writing full-time. She now lives in Salt Lake City, Utah, with her husband and their three children. Her favorite day of the week is Friday because often there is pizza for dinner.

www.jessicadaygeorge.com
@JessDayGeorge

Don't miss the magic of fantasy and fairy tale from

Jessica Day George!

www.jessicadaygeorge.com

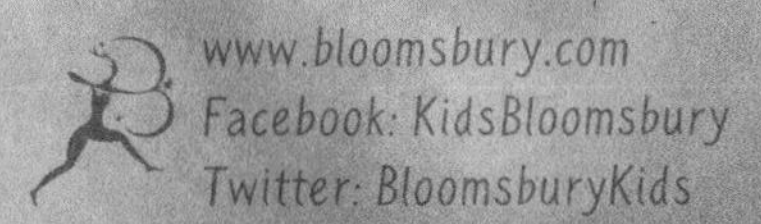